True Believer

Virginia Euwer Wolff lives in Oregon City, Oregon. She is
the author of several books for children and young adults
including *Probably Still Nick Swansen*, *The Mozart Season*
and *Bat 6*. *True Believer* is the second novel about
LaVaughn, her family and community. The first, *Make
Lemonade*, was published by Faber in 1995, and the author
is currently at work on a third.

True Believer was shortlisted for the Carnegie Medal
in 2001.

by the same author

Make Lemonade

TRUE BELIEVER
Virginia Euwer Wolff

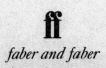

faber and faber

First published in Great Britain in 2001
by Faber and Faber Limited
3 Queen Square London WC1N 3AU
First published in the USA
by Atheneum Books for Young Readers
an imprint of Simon & Schuster Children's Publishing Division

A CIP record for this book
is available from the British Library

ISBN 0–571–20742–1 (cased)
0–571–20702–2 (pbk)

10 9 8 7 6 5 4 3

for Marilyn E. Marlow

Acknowledgements

Thanks to Anthony Wolff; Juliet Wolff; Gene Euwer; Mary Gunesch; Artrille Coleman; Lawson Fusao Inada; Jann Lingren; the Rev. Tim Haley; the staff of the Gladstone Library; Susie Bacon, Family Services Coordinator, Doernbecher Children's Hospital; Francine Warner, St. Hilda's and St. Hugh's School; and most earnestly to Brenda Bowen.

Part One

1

My name is LaVaughn and I am 15.

When a little kid draws a picture
it is all a big face
and some arms stuck on.
That's their life.

Well, then:
You get older
and you are a whole mess of things,
new thoughts, sorry feelings,
big plans, enormous doubts,
going along hoping and getting disappointed,
over and over again,
no wonder I don't recognize
my little crayon picture.
It appears to be me
and it is
and it is not.

2

In the sex class we have to take by school law
where they showed condoms and scared us about AIDS,
they said, "Sexuality is the most confusing thing
about being a teenager." I am sure
this is correct
because I strained my ears to hear over the racket
of kids making a joke of the class,
waving condoms on their fingers,
hooting.
And also because the sex teacher said it four times.

But me and my friends Myrtle & Annie
say it don't have to be the most confusing.
There is math and other hard subjects too
and street murders right near your block,
even people you loved.
And also torment of being let down
by what you counted on.
Me and Myrtle & Annie could say 1,000 examples.

The thing to do is stay virgin.

Then you don't have to wonder if you're pregnant
or worry about being a bad person
or decide whether to have the baby or abort it
or wonder for the rest of your life
if the baby is healthy
in her adopted home. Or his.

Me and Myrtle & Annie,
we all want to save our bodies for our right husband
when he comes along.

There is several ways to do this saving.
One is be snarly nasty to boys and not be their friend
and they will stay away from you.
But there is this girl everybody knows about,
she hated boys and men of all kinds
and one day she got raped just by going
to the discount store, she is a wreck you pity,
she slides her back along the locker doors in the hallways
and has lurching eyes.

Another way is Cross Your Legs for Jesus.
This is the club Myrtle joined, and Annie will probably too.
For the club you memorize Bible verses,
and in the club you will go to Hell if you have unmarried sex.
The club has many retreats and parties and fun picnics.
Boys are in it too.

The third way is never go anywhere by yourself.
I believe in my heart each of these 3 are not for me.
Be nasty to all boys and men?

No. I like them.
And it didn't work for that poor girl.

And Cross Your Legs for Jesus seems like a good idea at first.
But it doesn't feel right
when I think about it.
Does Jesus want that droopy raped girl to go to Hell?

And number 3 is trouble from beginning to end.
Never go anywhere alone? Sometimes I like to be alone.
To think.

I don't know how you recognize your own special husband
when he comes along. Will he look
totally different? Or does he look like everybody else
and you're the only one to recognize him?

I sure would like to get kissed.
How that would feel on my mouth.
How different I would be after,
a changed climate down in my insides.

3

And another thing.
My mom sat me down last night and she said,
"Verna LaVaughn. You remember your college plans."
This was not a question. She used both my names.

"Sure, I remember." This is too offhand for her
and she snaps at me about my tone of voice.
She has radar,
can feel rudeness coming, also sarcasm
before they start.
Also fake tiredness when you don't want to answer.
With my mom you are alert at attention or nothing.
"Yes, I remember my college plans," I say, polite.

"Well, you make sure you do.
Because I got a better job offer, I'll quit this mere little job
if you're sure you remember about college.
This job pays more,
I can put more in your college account.
It has better health benefits and dental."
And she says she'll have night meetings,

and for sure more paperwork. "I have to know," she says.
"Will you make me proud I took this big jump?

"Put yourself in my place, LaVaughn.
More of me goes to the office, less of me can stay home.
You understand?"

Sure, I'm happy for her new job.
This might mean I'd have more room to myself
without her standing over me
watching my own personal judgment.
"I understand," I say back.

"I don't think so.
You know what this means?
This means you can't do anything
real
dumb,
LaVaughn."
She looks at me with her face full of rules.

I know the rules, have always known them.
Go to school, do homework,
have safe friends,
have a job after school,
don't make bad decisions.
When I baby-sat for that Jolly
with her two babies and no husband
was a bad decision my mom thought,
but I come out of that with no harm done,

and I also helped Jolly get up
after what her life done to her.
And those little kids were so cute, I miss them still.

"'Cause I can't pull you out of any mess, Verna LaVaughn,"
my mom aims her eyebrows at me.
"You got your work to do,
I got mine. There's only just so much of me
to go around."

At this moment I love my mom real much
knowing so much of her has been going around me
my whole life.
Then in the next minute she says,
"I seen many youngsters change their minds,
forgetting their life plan
or they pretend they never had one.
You need a long memory, LaVaughn.
You can't go forgetting the minute it gets too hard."

I say I know that.
We agree I still mean it about college.
I tell her I appreciate her.
And I truly believe
those things are both completely true.

And three hours go by till she starts again.
I'm in bed, still awake.
She comes in and sits on the edge
and she says,

"And another thing.
"You know what would stop your college plans
for sure, LaVaughn."

This too is not a question.
I'm supposed to know. I can think of many things,
money first of all.
Or a deadly accident on the street, her getting fired,
me getting low grades,
all the disasters that happen in many varieties
to people just trying to go along.

"A baby," she says.
"Oh!" I say, in huge surprise. "Not me. For sure. Promise."
"So you say now," she says.
"Promises are easy to break," she says.
"People get confused.
You can't do that, LaVaughn.
You can not let yourself get confused.
You know what I mean?"

"Mom," I say, "I'm not confused."
"People are confusable," she goes on.
"You keep your eyes on college.
I tell you this, LaVaughn:
What's down there between a person's legs
gets them into more trouble than anything."

This is embarrassing. I don't want to hear her opinion.
"I'm counting on you like I never counted on anybody
since your dad was here."

I tell her she can count on me.
We say Goodnight
and I am relieved my mom is out of my own private room
with her depending and counting on
and warnings.

I have hopes for life and some love too
and surprises.
After a long time I go to sleep
and dream of dancing
with somebody, nobody clear, just vague
with his arms around me.
And he likes the real LaVaughn in me.

4

I am lucky,
born under a good star, maybe.

Of the bad things that happened
the worst, top of the list of all time, is my dad got killed
when I was so little.
It is a burden like they say.
And nobody, my mom nor nobody
knows how this private burden weights on me.

But at least I had a dad. And he loved me gigantically.
In the picture on my bedroom wall,
holding a little version of me in his arms,
we are in matching baseball caps,
that is a happy man grinning.

And my friends. I am lucky in them.
Myrtle & Annie, they were with me
all the way through.
Myrtle and me were helpful to Annie all we could be
when she had that divorce in second grade,

and then the second divorce too,
in sixth.
And the way Myrtle's family takes drugs is a crime.
Very often she did not even want to go home.
Till her father went to rehab
when we were in eighth grade,
he is in there again now, too.
He promised Myrtle he would make it this time.
Still, she holds her breath.
Me and Annie are sympathetic.
But sympathy won't make her life different.

My friend Jolly got things complicated last year,
Myrtle & Annie rolled their eyes
about her. Jolly couldn't help it. I kept telling them.
It wasn't her fault she was pregnant
before she was old enough to see straight.
It was a dangerous world she got born into
with hardly never a chance for niceness in her life.

But when Myrtle & Annie got cleaning jobs at the church
and got invited into the Jesus club there,
first Myrtle, then Annie,
they acted like Jolly was dirt down beneath them.
Then Jolly ended up a slight hero
so they were wrong about her,
even if they never said so.

But they are still loyal to me for life, and me to them.
We don't have to say it in words, it just is.
It's true the pavement around here is filthy from side to side,

the alleys reek
and they are full of deadly events that could happen any minute.
High school students shoot their classmates
and if you even take one glance at the science of the world
you would want to never get out of bed in the morning,
birds and beasts are going extinct,
the rivers are poison, the fish are dying,
there is dangerous rain.

But I have these friends,
and my mom even took a harder job so I can get out of here
when I'm grown up.

And my hope is strong like an athlete.
Every morning when we walk through the metal detectors
to get into school
I know in my heart it may feel like a day of just waiting in lines
and hearing bells ring
and watching teachers try to keep order
among those wrongdoers in the classes.
But.
It is an important day
of dues-paying so I can go to college and be out of here.
I'll pay.

5

And I am lucky to have a room of my own,
instead of sleeping on a fold-out
like Annie in her house.

My room is my private territory
complete with my special ceiling design.

My ceiling above my bed is cracked like a tree hanging over,
and last summer when I was restless one rainy day
I painted branches on,
and put a bird nest up there too
and little baby birds peeking out
with their eensy skinny feathers
and their all-mouth look like on a science show.
I used my watercolors from way back in childhood,
my 10th birthday present from the aunts.
The set has six different greens
and enough odd hues and shades
to do branches and a good tree trunk.
I am quite proud of my painting.
Well, my mom came home and saw the wall and ceiling

and her mouth went into shock
as a rent-payer.
"Oh, LaVaughn, look what you did," she says,
"Oh, no," she says, and "Oh, no," again,
while she catches her breath and thinks.

Then she calmed down.
She stood on different spots in my room,
at the corner of my desk,
and by the closet door,
and over by the wastebasket.
She climbed on my chair and took a look up close,
and she laid down on my bed to see it from there,
never saying a word, just shifting around and looking.

At the end of this short tour of my room which is not large
her face got patienter
and she said, "LaVaughn, that's nice,
that's so nice. Oh, LaVaughn, that's real, real nice."
And she says in a whisper,
"Your dad would be proud."

It made the lump come in my throat
that came before lots of times
when I'm wondering how it would feel with his arms around me
like before when I was so little.
Sometimes I think I can almost make the feeling.
And then it disappears.

I tell my mom thanks.

6

Myrtle & Annie sing their club song for me before gym.

> *"I gave my heart to Jesus,*
> *God's kingdom will endure.*
> *He gives to me my energy,*
> *Jesus keeps me pure."*

Then the chorus goes "Cross your legs for Jesus," and it repeats.

They say it sounds better with guitar and drums.
They are obvious about how unsaved I am.
They have new "JESUS LOVES YOU" shoelaces, bright gold.

We do our warm-ups,
then we go through the volleyball formations,
we holler and huff and jump like we are taught,
and it might look like old times
among Myrtle & Annie and me, but it's not.
"You're missing out on the miracle, LaVaughn,"
says Myrtle, in the showers.

I am not innocent enough to ask what miracle she means.
It is the miracle of being saved by God from being a sinner.

I didn't want to argue.
I imagine there is a God out there, or a Something.
Something to get the whole thing spinning along
way back there before there was anything
to even have a shape to it.

Myrtle & Annie and me went all through this subject before.
But now they have new news.
Myrtle & Annie say all Muslims and Jews and Hindus
and other religions will go to Hell
along with criminals and sexual teenagers
and all tribes of foreign lands
that have not come to Jesus and the Bible
which they say God wrote.
They don't explain how God came out of the sky
and wrote down words. "You just don't get it, LaVaughn."

It is the Joyful Universal Church of Jesus
that tells them these things.
They are right: I don't get it.
I personally would like to know how God let my dad die.
And why hasn't God made Myrtle's father
get well from drugs yet?
That would be a miracle.

Me and Myrtle share a bottle of shampoo like always
and I look back and forth at them
as we dry ourselves and put on our clothes.

With their club coming between our friendship
I want to say, "Yes! I'll be in your club!"

But I don't do it,
it doesn't feel right.
I don't think that is the job of Jesus, to keep me pure.
And I don't mean to be mean to Jesus in my thoughts,
that little baby born in a manger.
But I don't get how he hates so many millions of people
and sends them down to Hell.

So as we are getting dressed
and I run Annie's comb
down the back of her hair like always
for her exactly equal braids she wants,
I am wondering is this the last time I will ever have
Annie's comb in my hand, going down her hair.
I keep my eyes on the back of Annie's head,
bisecting her hair precisely.

And my skin goes shivery for a moment.
I want to join with them
to have it be like the old times we had,
but there's something holds me back.
If there is a God and Jesus,
is my dad in their heaven up there?
And if there isn't,
where is he?
Can he see me?

7

And then the biggest surprise:
Suddenly here comes Jody back again, changing everything.

He lived here a long time ago, then he left
and now he comes back, an astonishment in the elevator.

When we were little we played
kick-the-can a kazillion times.
We went to each other's messy little birthdays
and spilled ice cream
and I remember like a movie
how I stole his party hat one time,
it was blue and I was grabby.

Jody and me
were the only ones that got punished
when all of us kids on our side of the building
were mean to a person in a wheelchair. Some of the big kids
wheeled her very fast over big gashes in the sidewalk.
Us little ones just watched, but that was bad enough.

My mom was mad. Jody's too.

"You like to stare at people that had bad luck, LaVaughn?
Verna LaVaughn, you like to stare
at that poor woman being tormented?
What else you like to do, LaVaughn? Huh?"

I told her I like to color in coloring books.
She took away every coloring book I had,
and the crayons and markers too
for a whole month. "That will teach you," she said.

She put them away in her closet
and I couldn't color till she took them out again.

Jody was not allowed to ride his bike for a week.
Nobody else got punished.

Jody's mom and my mom taught us cards,
we played Hearts in their apartment and Old Maid.
And Double Solitaire.
Our mothers traded keys, one for each of us,
hanging on a string
so us little ones would have a safe place
to go in emergencies.
Even with self-defense classes in the building
you still need a place to go in danger.
It is a rule of the Tenant Council.

Jody and me each used our keys on strings
once way back then. Trying them out.
He came to our house
when I was just learning to make a peanut butter sandwich.
I made two of them, he ate most of his.

And I used the key in their lock one time.
He showed me his tropical fish in a tank,
he knew the big long names of those bright-colored swimmers.
We traded comic books and never gave them back.

Once Jody and me played cards for 2 days
when it snowed and there was no school.

And then they moved away.

And now they're back again.
And this is such a weird miracle about my little childhood pal:
He is suddenly beautiful.

In the elevator, it's all I can do to say his name.
"Jody?" I say. I steady myself against the elevator wall
in case it is not him. And because he is too gorgeous
to look at head-on.
He doesn't remember me
and then he does. "You were good at kick-the-can," he said.
"Really?" I said.
"Yeah, you had good legs," says this brand-new old person.
"Thanks," I say. "Do you still have fish in a tank?"
I'm amazed at my normal sound,
talking so calm to such beauty.

He could be in movies,
the way the parts of his face go together.

His mouth moves and words come out, Yes,
he still has fish, his hand goes to the elevator button,

I follow it, the wrist, thumb, index finger, a button pushes,
his arm goes back where it was.
My chest is so full of heartbeats it jolts my thinking.

Somewhere he was getting to be a perfect, handsome person
while I was only going through the years.
In the elevator maybe I asked him where he has been,
maybe not.
His face is standing there looking straight into mine,
the shape of his mouth, oh,
I can't imagine I ever saw such a boy before
and yet it is still the face of Jody from back then.
I get out of the elevator at my floor
and I lean on the wall,
my heart too loud for comfort
and my brain not so level either.

8

I get my whole breath back
by the time my mom comes home.
She is not struck dumb by the news.
She reminds me what I was not paying attention to
when I was a kid, the reason why they left:
Jody's mom moved them away
to try to get Jody a better chance in life.
"That woman, she's exhausted, she's drained,
cleaning dirty houses day in, day out,
Jody's all she's got."

I make comparison with Jody's mom and mine
but it is not the same at all. My mom never
cleaned other people's houses.
She would not live such a beat down life,
she just would not.
"Well, they tried, she couldn't pay that higher rent,
she got farther behind all the time,
and. . . ." My mom plunks her paperwork on the counter,
reaches over and rubs a sponge around the sink,

lets her breath out in a huff.
". . . and here they are, back again."

She says in her emphasizing voice:
"She was the first one when your dad died.
The very first one.
She come up here with a casserole,
she brought Jody along,
she stayed with me the whole night."

That is all a fog to me. Maybe I didn't notice him,
so confused as I was.
I'll never know how my mom made it through that time.
"You be nice to Jody, LaVaughn.
They don't have it easy."

So that's the way it is about Jody.
And she's telling me to be nice to him.
Does she not even know what Jody looks like?
I look at her flat as a plate, no expression.
I say Sure, I'll do that.

Jody's back just in time to start the new school year.
My heart is clunking.

9

They trade extra keys again,
my mom and Jody's mom,
for the safety of Jody and me.
This is hard to notice with a straight face.
And at first I was much too silenced by looking at him
to say anything.
Then it's the elevator again.
One day he swings around the corner on a skateboard,
zooming in through the door
the last instant before it closes
and he quick-turns, throws me an orange
and says, "Hi, LaVaughn, buddy,
how's your life?" His face so bright with energy.

There he is, rocking almost invisibly
on the skateboard
and asking me that question.

I answer with something not enough.
Some stumbled words.

Maybe I said, "Uh, OK."
Or maybe I said, *you are too gorgeous*
I can't look at you and talk to you at the same time.
He gets off at his floor,
disappears, & then waves one hand back in the doorway
and quick pulls it out again.
And is gone.

The elevator smells like chlorine.

10

I straighten my room, run the dust mop under my bed.
I wash the kitchen counter,
I scrub the bathroom floor.

I clear away all the mess on my desk
for a neat place to study. I put the orange there.

Jody said I used to have good legs
and he called me buddy
and he gave me that orange.

I take off my jeans
and stand on a chair
and look at my legs in the mirror.
I turn around every which way, I bend over
even though I have my own personal legs memorized
like any normal person.
I look at my flesh new now.

I get out boxes of stuff from the closet,
I'm hunting for a class picture
from when Jody used to be here.

I have odd scary feelings down there on the floor
looking through the boxes. Some little thing
makes me queasy.

Under many papers and small gloves
and a sweater and 3 sets of jacks,
it turns up in a big envelope that has an old-paper smell,
the photograph of all 37 of us way back then,
it must be 4th grade.
There is Jody, a skinny little kid
with his arm around that Victor
we all used to like so much
—that was my queasiness. Victor.
I haven't thought about him in so long.
I get the jitters there on the floor in my room.

I quick look away from Victor.
There's our teacher
that had us make the big Valentine Box
and we all got Valentines and had candy
and Myrtle dropped hers in the snow.
That teacher had us sing songs, "A-Bi-Yo-Yo"
and "This Land Is Your Land" and "We Shall Overcome."
She had some hairs on her face
and she never yelled,
even when some kids were terrible.

And there's the other children too that are gone:
Robby and Timothy,
Arnulfo and Jorge and Shyrelle.
They would be 15 this year
with us,

yelling on the sidewalk,
eating and sleeping and going to the bathroom
and getting report cards
and getting in trouble,
but they are not. Every one of them
is not alive anymore.
Arnulfo in the house fire,
Jorge in the bus accident,
Robby ran in the way of his mother's pimp,
and Shyrelle got held in front of her big brother
when the gang gun went off
and she lived for 6 days
before dying of all that violence and dumbness.

And Victor. Jody's best friend.
Victor was the comical one,
he built the funniest Lego contraptions I ever saw
and he made up whole stories to go with them.
Victor that got caught with dope in fifth
and our teacher cried about it.
Victor that everybody loved for his jokes,
we all got scared of his knife in sixth,
Victor that was dead that same year, buried in a cemetery,
I don't know if anybody goes to visit him there or not.

And there's Myrtle & Annie and me in the second row.
I remember that green sweater, my aunts gave it to me.
We are such cute little kids there,
we do not seem any more alive
than Victor and the others,
but look at us now.

11

Well, here's the reason about the chlorine.
I found out the night of the fire,
not a big blaze,
only one fire truck came and nobody died,
and Jody and me were there among the onlookers.
I'm getting used to him being here
and I can say brief things to him
before my heart gets too hysterical to go on.

Firefighters are rushing around,
red lights are twirling,
and Jody is helping some little kid get his dog untangled
where the leash is looped around a parking meter.
The dog is howling with one leg caught in the strap
and the noise of sirens and shouting
and little kids crying
reminds you how much you hate it here,
and Jody is showing the little kid so patient
how to unwind the leash and he talks gentle to the dog
and I say Hi. Jody says Hi back to me

at the same time he puts the little kid's hat back on
that fell off in the confusion.

I asked Jody about the chlorine smell
and he explained,
his face all shiny in the ambulance light:
It's because he swims. All the time.
At a pool way far away, he takes two buses
or he goes on his skateboard in good weather.
Before school, after school, on weekends.
And he cleans the pool, cleans the locker rooms,
does maintenance. To pay for coaching
in diving and swimming.

And he says he's going to college too.
That is a mysterious coincidence,
two people in the same dirty building
both going to college
when nobody here ever did that before.

Jody is even more greedy about it than I am,
he can't wait
to get out of here. "There's gotta be
something better than this," he says to me.

I tried a joke: "Your skateboard is gonna take you
out of here?" Jody is serious.
"I'm gonna swim out."

He was only gorgeous till I heard this.
Now he's blunt determined on top of it.
I tell him, "Me too.

32

I'm saving money, and my mom too,
I had such a baby-sitting job last year,
I'm going to go to college too. Really."

"Good for you, LaVaughn," he says with his beautiful mouth.
He's more reachable now
and it makes me feel like partners with him
in something.

Colleges have scholarships for swimming
and they pay for your schooling
if you swim for their team.
I never knew about such a thing but he says it's true.

Somebody Jody's mom cleans house for
found out about him, how he could swim so good.
They took him to their club and a coach watched him
and Jody got onto the team.
That was just about the whole conversation
but by it I learned his schedule of daily life.

Well, Annie is not so excited he came back.
I knew she would not be.
Because Jody did a childhood good deed
but Annie always believed he brought on her second divorce
all because he saw her first stepfather
sprawled in a doorway
and ran to get help.

And they took Annie's first stepfather away
in the ambulance.
They pumped his stomach

and that was the last straw for Annie's mom,
her own second husband drunk in a doorway
in front of little children
and she divorced him.

Then a social worker came
to see if Annie's mom was taking good care
of Annie and her sister
and they threatened to send them both
into Foster Care if she made one little mistake.
It was horrible for Annie.

She liked that stepfather,
he was just a peaceful drunk,
he only ever hit her once,
and that was by accident.
Annie resented Jody for making trouble.
We never talk about it anymore,
but we all know Annie's mother's name is in a file
and those social workers
could come again.

Myrtle is on the other hand. She liked Jody
and was partners with him in social studies
back in fifth.
Their group did the best report on Egypt,
they showed how the brains got sucked out
through the nose of the mummy.
I bet every single person in that whole class
remembers it to this day, the ones that are still alive.
It was so stunning about the brains of the mummies.

Annie even has a class with Jody now,
and she still doesn't like him
for that old reason from long ago.
"I don't trust him, he has a shifty face,
he is not regular," she says.

Me, I often inhale the chlorine smell in the empty elevator
and my whole body goes twang.

12

I go to the first meeting of Grammar Build-Up
like my last year's teacher told me twice I should.
She caught me in Hallway A at the beginning of September.
"You sign up for Grammar Build-Up like I told you?"
she shouts over the crowd.
"I don't know when it is," I holler back.
She squeezes through and says into my ear,
"They put it after school, find Auxiliary Schedule B,
where it says Tutorials,
I don't know why they make these things so complicated.
You go to Room 304 right after school today.
You tell the teacher I sent you. It's Dr. Rose.
She'll sign your Elective Card, you go to that class."
OK, I tell her. "It's a doctor?"

"Not a medical one.
You stay with that tutorial, you won't be sorry," she says.
I say OK and we turn our separate ways through the noise.
So I go there after school. I have seen Jody twice today.
Whole bursts of energy almost bounce me along.

This Dr. Rose is tall and very good manners looking,
she wears a don't-mess-with-me suit
and very tiny shiny earrings in her ears.
She eyeballs each of the 13 of us
and we get quiet.

She opens her mouth. She says,
long and slow enough
to make people shift their eyes away from her,
like it is a word of greatness,
" L A N G U A G E . "
She scans the room to see us looking away from her
and there is not a sound.
In that quiet she goes on, very slow,
"Settle yourselves.   Compose yourselves.   Get ready to learn.
By tomorrow you will be   ready to learn   when you step
over that threshold,"   she points her long arm behind her
to the door we just come in.
"Today is day one.   Today is your introduction."
She looks us over with superior eyes.

"This is an after-school tutorial,
but do not be misled by that.
Do not even begin to think you'll drop in
                              when you feel like dropping in.
Do not even begin to think you will do the lessons
                              when the mood strikes you.
Do not even begin to think you will
                              dillydally about your work here.
Now: Why are you here, young man?"

She has pointed her eyes toward a slumped boy.
"I want to be a senator," he says, barely hearable.
Her eyes go around watching our reactions,
which there aren't any
among us motionless bodies.
I don't want her eyes pointing into me like that.

"And you, young woman?" Her eyes go to the girl behind me.
"I'm here so I can talk good for TV, which I want to go into."

"And you, young man?" She means the boy in front of me.
"I want to rise above myself," he says.
By this time nobody in this room would laugh,
this teacher has us all on some kind of strings
attached to the waves of her voice.
Her eyes come to me.
"And you?"
My voice comes out puny. "I was sent here
by my last year's teacher
to get improved."

Dr. Rose breathes in very deep, her jacket swells just an iota,
and she says, "We have a multitude
of obstacles to overcome here.
We'll begin."

She says, "Nouns name the world. Adjectives qualify it.
Verbs are our meager attempt to record
the vast motion of all life,
prepositions connote the relationships among phenomena.
Does any of you know what I'm talking about?"

I shake my head slightly
and I see every head in the room doing the same.
"Well," she says.

We have to have a special notebook just for this class,
no stray pieces of paper falling out of it
from anywhere else.
And we have to do our work in pen, not pencil.
She gives us a diagram of a sentence
that has slanted lines and branches.
She announces:
She will instruct us
for precisely one-fourth of the class time each day.
We will work in pairs for precisely one-fourth.
Another fourth of the class we will drill in groups of four.
And the fourth fourth we will be tested on what we learned.

"We shall begin with case.
How many of you know what is meant by case?"
Nobody raises a hand.
"Before you leave this room today,
you will understand 'This is I' and 'That is he.'"

And she hands out a list of I-my-me,
you-your-yours-you,
he-she-it-his-her-hers-its-him-her-it.
And she shows where to memorize
and says we have to know by tomorrow
how to answer the phone
and how to point out each other, "That is she, this is I"
and do it correct every time.

My partner is Ronell.
She got pushed into it by a teacher too,
who said Ronell will not get to realize her specialness
if she doesn't get to go to college
and make a better world some way.

We do sentences to each other and we make mistakes
and Dr. Rose shows us our mistakes on the paper.
She makes us do it over again right.
After we do this for a while we get to rest for 3 minutes.

This is dizzying, and the teacher knows it, and she says
in her exact voice,
"Some of you   will   invent   excuses
not to come to this after-school elective class.
You will find other endeavors
that are more   immediately   gratifying.
The rest of you will struggle
and be   exalted   in your learning.
And, by the way, you will become taller,
should you choose to remain."

She takes another deep breath.
"In this room are fewer than   one   percent
of the students in this school.
Be aware that you are the one per cent.   Good day."

And she flutters her long fingers up,
meaning we should get up out of our seats and leave.
We do it.

Outside the door
me and Ronell and four others roll our eyes
and we laugh all quiet,
not a sound, just six stumbling bodies
going up the hallway,
all bent over with laughter,
trying not to have our sinuses pop,
even 2 of us were boys.

Me and Ronell agree
we will go back for more.

13

Well, my plan from before
looks so little scrimpy now.
It looked so big when I was a littler girl.
It was I was going to go to college
and get a job, get out of here
and not live with garbage and stink on my street
and nasty criminals in the neighborhood,
shooting. And also get married someday
and later have a pretty baby.

But that was like that little kid's drawing: You know?
A lopsided head and big long arms
reaching out to you don't know where?
Now there are good parts added.

In my room my school books are all lined up
on the bookcase I had for years,
since the time I first thought about going to college,
way back in fifth grade.
My mom found a 3-shelf bookcase
abandoned on the sidewalk and she dragged it home.

She put the loose middle shelf back in with nails
and we painted the whole thing shiny blue, my choice.
It was the first furniture I ever got to paint.

And the books in it are crowded now.
There's no room for my new notebooks and folders.
When I cleaned my room
in such excitement over Jody in the elevator
I put them on the floor in 4 neat stacks.

Folders on my floor,
a bird nest on my ceiling,
my room is almost how I want it.
I think of how Myrtle & Annie are slipping away from me
and I keep remembering
us three were laying on my bed
admiring my birds and the leaves on my ceiling tree,
and Myrtle said she wanted me to paint a picture on her ceiling,
only she never decided exactly what she wanted,
maybe a beach but I didn't think I could do good waves,
and I never painted her a picture at all.

Now I wonder if I ever will.
Not if they go out of my life to be all the property of Jesus
and I am not in their club.

So: In my heart there is discontrolled excitement
about Jody, how he brightens up this ugly neighborhood
and also severe sadness about Myrtle & Annie leaving me,
but the three of us still have fun in gym,
the only class we have together besides science.

I think it is because we get to jump around.
It feels somewhat like how it used to be
but those feelings are deceiving.

And at the same time I am sort of praying to a sort of God
I don't know exists
out there in space or inside my mind or wherever,
that rehab works this time for Myrtle's dad,
so he will stay clean
and watch Myrtle grow up and finish school.
And I am adding could Jody like me like I like him.

And in my plan is the Grammar class now too.
My Grammar Tutorial study group
has Ronell, Doug, and Artrille.
They are all one year older than me.
It is actually fun doing those drills,
because Artrille makes it a game.
He got us to bring hats to class.
Mine is a sun hat of my mom's,
it has a big fuchsia pink ribbon hanging down,
and Doug has a cowboy hat.
Artrille's hat is a hard helmet like for building construction
and Ronell's baseball cap says "Woman" in great big letters.
We do our drills wearing our hats,
and for some reason it helps me remember better.
We call ourselves the Brain Cells, we have team huddles,
and a team clutch, with all eight of our hands
in a stack in the middle. It is a small club I like
with these people who would be strangers if I didn't know them.
I privately want Ronell's legs

44

and she privately wants my waistline.
We imagine trading.

Artrille is the one who said the very first day
he wanted to rise above himself.
I give him credit for saying that right out loud,
knowing he might get things thrown at him
in any other class but this one.

There is a subjunctive we are learning.
"LaVaughn, it would be advisable
that you remove your waistline
and lay it on me," Ronell says in our drill.
I reply back, "I deem it mandatory
that you attach your legs to my person."
And Doug and Artrille go on
about how girls are never satisfied.
"We prefer that you not be patronizing
about LaVaughn and I,"
says Ronell, and the teacher is instantly there,
with her magnetic voice,
"about LaVaughn and me, objective case,"
and I'll never forget that one, due to the way her voice is.

My plan is still the same as always. Only bigger now.
Even when I took my mind off it for a while
I always came back to it, that plan to go to college.
Even more now. Because of Jody.
Sometimes he's there when I get off the bus,
skating by on his board: "Hey, LaVaughn!"
He is like a bright flag going past.

And he told me to turn all around in my Grammar hat
and he said it looked nice.
Eek, I didn't know what to do.
There must be a God or somebody out there
to bring Jody to my life. Don't you think?

At night I say Grammar exercises to myself:
The apartment keys belong to Jody and me.
                              Never "to Jody and I."
We little kids played kick-the-can.
                              Never "us little kids."
There are two times in a day I can see him.
                              Never "there is two times."

And I found a good dictionary at the Goodwill
and only 3 pages are torn
and it doesn't even smell like mildew or any other bad thing.
It says "Collegiate" on it
and I look at that word "Collegiate"
on the cover before I go to sleep
and I put my whole hands up in the air and I say YES!

14

The only thing missing from my plan was a job
till today.
My last year's employment my mom never did like,
but working for Jolly was in reality a very good job.
When I baby-sat Jeremy and Jilly,
those accidental babies of hers,
with their cuteness and their awful messiness—
those kids were a good thing for me,
along with their abandoned mother Jolly.
She'd be a lesson for anybody about not getting pregnant.

This year I need a job that won't use me up so much.
And it has to earn money for my college account
that is growing all the time
with little tiny amounts of interest.

So back to the job bulletin board I go,
we're already in the second week of school.
I am not so talented to have a pool job
like Jody, but there is some things I can do. Are.

Many janitor jobs were posted there,
and greasy-food. And part-time clerical,
and market research interviewing,
and about 20 other things.
Naturally the school cafeteria always has their sign up
because people quit all the time.

Among this variety my eye hit the business card tacked up,
a light blue border around it,
just a child in a wheelchair,
a cutout shape of such a child,
and "The Children's Hospital."
A clenching happened in my heart.
I wrote the number down.

I called them, they asked me questions,
I went up the hill after school for my interview.
The hospital is huge, the lobby has children's paintings
and animal sculptures and many carved birds hanging.
The elevator is like a big room, I went to the 12th floor.

The interviewing office has children's handprints
across the walls, marching all in a row.
The interviewing woman asked me
if I'm responsible and punctual
and can I handle details, and I tell her yes to all of those.
Then she stared at me.
"Do you *really like* children?" she said.
I told her about Jeremy and Jilly last year.

She told me this:
"Every child in our hospital

is the most important child in the world.
Some of them die here.
Everything we do is crucial.
There are liver transplants,
there is brain stem glioma,
children here are living, dying, staying, going."
I told her I would try my hardest to do my job right.
They hired me.
It is only working in laundry. And it is important.

I fold laundry and stack it and distribute it where it has to go.
And there is always the thought of those little children
laying on those sheets
so I fold them very nice, very, very nice.
And I feel like I am doing some good.
Folding sheets is not the biggest good in the world.
But it is some.

My heart is so happy with Jody
coming back so gorgeous and liking me—
I've got to do some good for somebody or I'll burst.

15

We went to get Myrtle a cat.
The Head Shepherd in the Jesus Club made a speech
on how a pet is the best thing
if you want somebody to love and sleep with.
And everybody in her whole section voted
they would get a cat or a dog.
Animal Rescue has so many unwanted orphan animals
that would be put to death if nobody takes them.

The kitten Myrtle picked is orange and white striped,
silky and staring, a very snuggling female
and she comes with a free coupon to get spayed.
We got a litter box set up and she introduced Peaches,
the name she gave it,
to her house
and it was all quiet over there,
with her dad away in rehab.

Annie is not able to get one for her mother's allergies.
And I would love a cat but not the cat smell.

Too much of it is in my building anyway.
It is sickening.

I'm glad we went together to the Animal Rescue
because it felt like back when we were kids
so little and short and so hopeful about everything.
We used to look in pet shops
with such childish longing.

I went all afternoon
not saying Jody's name out loud. For Annie's sake
I kept buttoning my lip the whole time.

And I looked in the eyes of them
and wished I could have everybody together
all liking each other
like the picture in my mind
of how we would all be.
I didn't feel right keeping my mouth shut
with these two old friends, it was unnatural.
We get the kitten all set up and not so scared,
and it's time to go our different ways.

"Well, we have to get ready for the club meeting,"
says Myrtle. "Too bad you don't want to join, LaVaughn."
They have matching Jesus bracelets and keychains.

I went to the hospital and folded sheets
remembering how worse it is for those children
than my little problems

and then I went home
and I laid down on my bed,
curling my arms around the pillow
pretending it was Jody
and looked up at my ceiling tree and birds' nest
and felt sorry for myself
alternating with feeling heavenly about Jody
for a whole long time.

Jittery at the bus stop with him,
or in the elevator
or walking into school with him,
sneaking a look sideways at him,
words coming out of my mouth clumsy
and my armpits sweating:
Is that perfect?

Or is it almost better being alone in my room imagining?
How he would put his arms all the way around me?

I couldn't figure out any answer to that,
So I got up and had dinner and did my homework.

16

They changed my science class at school.
A man from Guidance came in and talked to the teacher
and next thing I know they both tell me
I'm supposed to be in a different room.
It's true that class was too easy and way too loud,
but Myrtle & Annie are in it,
almost my last chance to be with them.

And suddenly I'm supposed to know mitosis of the cells
and how to draw their divisions on paper
including pairs of chromosomes.
I frankly never heard of any mitosis before
and it has patterns I never saw but they are so pretty,
but I don't let this show on my face.
I didn't recognize anybody in the new room,
but they give me a lab partner
and it turns out
he doesn't know anybody either. He just got switched too.

His name is Patrick,
he wears glasses and a green sweatshirt,

he talks at a slow rate of words.
He writes on a corner of his notebook page
and slides it over to me:

> *You new*
> *me too*
> *what do we do?*

I scribble very fast underneath:

> *Listen real hard.*

The teacher says, "LaVerne,
you never saw this Biology book before?"
I tell her no, and I say my name is LaVaughn.
She says, "Well, LaVaughn, you have some catching up.
You need to read all up to here," she goes flipping pages.
"You need to know mitosis by Tuesday, for the quiz."
She looks in my face and makes a change in her voice.
"Well," she nods me down close to where she is pointing,
"you just read all these for now, and save these—"
she pulls a rubber band off her wrist
and rubber-bands a bunch of pages—
"You save these for next week."
I tell her thanks.
She asks me which science class I just came from.
I tell her. She says, "Well, let's see if you can keep up."

I look around the room.
Different shoes. These students in this room

look very unfamiliar.
Even their hair conditioner smells different.

There are unbroken microscopes and equipment,
the teacher walks around and helps us,
and Patrick shows me things I don't know,
like prophase and metaphase, which he figured out already.

The Guidance man explains:
"LaVaughn, your records had us confused at first.
You need classes that'll get you ready for college.
But we didn't know that. Not at first.
But we know now. We know now."

I am glad they got me straight.
I ask him how they got me confused.
He says he's not sure.

That man said I should come see him in Guidance
if I have questions.
I don't have a clue what he means.
But I want to know:
If I do well in the new class like he says,
will that make me have a good life?
Will it make me get to college
and can I marry Jody in my future?
Those are not Guidance questions. Even I know that.

I'm thinking: Poor Myrtle & Annie.
Lucky Patrick, lucky me.

But they have Jesus.
But I have my new class.
Insects evolved wings 350 million years ago.
Bird bones have a honeycomb structure.
We have 98% the same genes as chimps and gorillas.
The synapses of that little Jeremy,
my sweet little baby-sitting boy from last year,
his synapses are already formed. He is 3.
Science is amazing. Patrick even says it's beautiful.

One thing for sure: It's so quiet in this room.
You can hear the teacher whenever you want to.
I think they even have more watts in the bulbs.

17

Patrick is super smart. He read our lab results
two different ways. I asked him which was right.
"Well, it's open to interpretation," says Patrick.
I did not ever know any 15-year-old that talked that way.

But he is even too friendly.
Already in the first week of Biology
he wanted to carry my books to Hallway D,
where we go to different stairs.

It was ridiculous. I said so.
He said, "I know that. Can I do it anyway?"
He doesn't have a snarly sound like lots of boys I know.
He takes a long time to say his words in his leisurely voice,
but he's just too friendly.
I have not seen him in a different shirt yet
and he wears a cross of Jesus on a neck chain every day.
And he can't spell his words even though
he learns things faster than I do.
He comes back to the lab every afternoon to do extra science.

I didn't let him carry my books, I carried them myself.
It was the very same day that I found in the Biology book
"fibrillate," the leaping thing my heart does
when Jody comes skateboarding by.

18

The Food & Flashlight Formal is coming,
posters are taped up in hallways and bathrooms.
I never went to a real dance before
where you wear a pretty dress and dance with a boy.

I can't not think about it
with new-old Jody living in my building,
going to school with me, leaving his chlorine smell
in places that catch me unsuspecting
like lunch line, where I whiffed it in front of me
and was too speechless to say hi.

It says at 10:00 P.M. they turn off all the lights
and everybody shines flashlights,
just imagine how glowing it would be.
I imagine Jody and me waving our lights around
and laughing, having a good time.

If he asked me to go to the dance with him
I wouldn't be shy at all.

The food part is you must bring a can of food for the poor.
There are many poor around here, even more than us.
And always food drives.
It is said the food we give the poor
only builds their strength to buy more drugs
but we keep doing it anyway.

At The Children's Hospital
I saw three crack babies already.
Maybe it is pregnant people on crack that get our food.
But if you don't give to the food drive,
what will they have to eat?

I am so excited about going to the dance with Jody
I would bring 50 cans of food.

I never did go on a date before.

I decorate my notebook covers with "Jody Jody Jody"
in fancy writing, full of loops and curves and wavy lines.
Jody, there is a dance and we could go to it together.

19

Myrtle & Annie won't even think of going.
Their club has its own party that night
and they're fluttery about it.
It's their Volleyball Volley over at the church where they meet.
The many Jesus clubs will play a tournament,
and they will have a movie called *Spirit of Faith Today*
full of bands and singers and saved people.
They'll have lots of food and sleep in sleeping bags on the floor.
God's Girls sleep in one big room
and God's Boys sleep in another, with assigned adults in charge.

I am hoping for a dress that is formal and unusual
and Myrtle & Annie are getting new pajamas
for the same night. They have new Jesus pillowcases.
They keep on inviting me
and I give them good credit for that,
just the same as I keep on making suggestions
about the Flashlight Formal
to them.
But maybe we are impossible friends now.
Myrtle has a photograph of her striped kitten
taped in her locker beside a big sticker, "On my way to heaven."
That animal is already half again as big as when she got it.

20

The instant I saw a huddle of kids
standing underneath the huge Food & Flashlight Formal poster
covered with canned food labels to advertise the dance
in Hallway A,
and there was Jody smack in the midst of them,
his head exactly under the foot
of the painted Jolly Green Giant and his peas,
I stopped in my tracks.

An alarm went off inside my chest,
shooting something like hot icicles all over me,
finger to foot,
Jody with all those girls and guys,
holding a close conversation and laughing
about some confidential thing.
I stopped sudden and caused a traffic tangle.
My head went all balloony with wanting to be in that bunch,
catching on to every bit of the joke.
I was shocked by how envy caught me up.
Jody might be asking one of those girls to the dance
right that instant

and my brain blazed.
I could laugh as good as any girl over there laughed
at whatever was funny,
and I stood there not hearing what they said
till I was pushed on in the crowd
to Biology
and I put my books down beside Patrick's pile
and I turned to the proper page about Linnaeus,
back 200 years ago, how he classified genus and species,
and I repeated in my mind:
mitochondria, cytoplasm, college, college, college.

I open my book to chromosomes
and Patrick is already working on the chart
about eukaryotes and prokaryotes.

He whispers to me in his slowpoke voice: "Hey, LaVaughn,
you know that dance they're having?
Will you go? With me?
The Food & Flashlight?
You want to?"

This is the first time
anybody ever asked me
to go on a date.
A little bell should ring.
Instead my hope folds up
with muttering disapointment
because it is only my lab partner,
not a real date boy,
and I know I have to say something to Patrick,

seeing his eyes bright and shiny,
waiting.

How do I do this?
I turn my page, find out I've gone past the proper part,
turn it back, look over at Patrick's page,
and time is going by and
he's still wearing the same green sweatshirt.
It feels like he's in my way,
a big rock in the road.
"Uh, I think I'm going with somebody."
It is rude and it is a lie.

I kept looking down at my book
and I felt flustered and fidgety,
wanting in all the diploid cells of me,
in all my chromatin threads
to go to that dance.
I wish Patrick would either be different
or go away.

Patrick says, "Oh." He looks down
at his lab notes and does not look up again.

21

Jody, there is a dance and we could go to it together.
What if he doesn't even know about the dance?

After folding laundry up at the hospital
I get home one evening at the same time he does,
I hear the skateboard and then
he scoots into the elevator just before it closes,
my arms bristle and my throat clinches.

Is he glad to see me? Yes. Not really. Yes. I don't know.
How can I say the right thing to such mystery eyes?
I ask, "Don't you get tired? All that swimming?"
He opens his face. "Oh, yeah, I get tired.
Trying to beat my own time in the butterfly.
Sure, I get tired.
But I've got my will. That's what you need.
I will get out of here." He is too beautiful to talk to.

"Me too," I say, and those 2 words are
all I can say before my mouth dries up

and I feel the stinky nervous breath coming.
The mouth bacteria love it when you feel insecure.

He goes on, maybe he didn't notice
I hardly even answered him.
He says, "You gotta have perspective.
And will. That's what you've got to have."

I start to say how smart he must be
to think it through like that,
but we are at his floor. He says,
"But hungry is the main thing.
After swimming.
I could eat a hundred chocolate chip cookies."
He skates out on his board. "So long, LaVaughn,"
and he's gone.

The dingy, scratched elevator
with terrible words scrawled,
and some of the buttons totally broken off,
you could feel sorry for the poor ugly thing,
but it is full of him and his wonderful chlorine smell.

Jody, there is a dance and we could go to it together.

22

It's payday at the hospital, and I go
to the Goodwill after work.

I know the Goodwill by heart.
Two of the workers have told me
about their life stories
of hard troubles and sickness
and their kids down on their luck. You can see
their poor lives, it even shows on their skin.
They often save shirts they think I might like.

This time I was just looking. Really.
But sometimes fate is there when you need it.
Partway down the third aisle,
there was the dress, pulled out from the rest
where somebody else must have looked at it and
then walked on.

It was perfect for me: dark blue ripply crushed velvet
with some little lace around the top.

It was the color I wanted, and the feel of it too.
The dress did not have a used smell to it.

I took it in the fitting room
where you don't want anything but your shoes
to touch the floor
where who knows what toxic microscopic things live.
You have to balance everything in your arms.

The dress looked like I would imagine
in my dreams of a dress,
except a place where some food was crusted
and a couple of mendable places in the back.

Well? Would I just up and buy this dress?
I had the money, it was waiting to jump out of my backpack.
I weighed the sides: If I bought it
and Jody did not ask me to go to the dance
it would hang wasted in my closet.
If I left it in the store and Jody did ask me to go to the dance
it might be gone when I come back. Somebody else
might wear it the very same night.

People came and went in the store,
mumbling, smelling, laughing,
confiding in strangers
while I thought it through.

I did it. I paid for the dress,
pretending it was just a normal purchase,

they put it in a bag
and I walked out
ready to borrow those shoes of Annie's
that already fit me
and I was all set for the dance.
Except.

All the way home
those wavy dreamy feelings kept coming
of how we'd dance together
how he'd look in some unexpected jacket,
a room full of music, a paradise to dance in.

How he would kiss me.

Those drifty feelings
took my mind off the Biology quiz the next day.
But I memorized lysosomes and the glucose formula
while I sponged the dress with liquid soap.

Patrick got 3 more points than I did
and I could feel the Guidance Man in my mind
asking me how come I did not get a perfect score like last week.
I shifted on my lab stool and bit my lip over the page
till it hurt.
Patrick explained me my mistake
like there was nothing wrong
like he did not ask me to the dance
like I didn't half-lie to him
like everything was fine.

We got to start an experiment
with fern spores in a Pepsi bottle terrarium
about alternation of generations.
The teacher came over
to check if we had our terrarium right
and she said how my quiz score went down today.
I felt her look right through my back
where I was leaning over the spores.
I couldn't look at Patrick
hunched over doing the lab report
and spelling his words wrong.

He evidently has another shirt, a brown one.

23

It looked like Jody caught on.
Early morning, near the metal detectors
at the door to school
he invited me—he invited me—
"Hey, LaVaughn, you want to go with me to the—"
I mentally had my new dress already on, and Annie's shoes,
I was ready to drape into his arms—
"—pool today? To practice my rescues.
For Lifeguarding. Lifeguard training."

I was making the Yes in my mouth already
and out it came, with my head nodding too much.
I was suddenly going to a swimming pool
to get nearly naked with Jody
and have him see my whole entire body shape and details.

One summer, a long time ago,
we got taught swimming lessons,
40 of us in a huge city pool.
The lifeguards blew whistles
and lined us up in groups,

the sun was so hot our feet burned.
We were little screamy children,
some bouncy and fat,
some of us bony with hangy swimsuits,
all of us splashing and gulping,
getting whistles blown at us
and trying to move our arms and legs right,
it was sink or swim,
a wild adventure
in 3 feet of shiny water.

Every different thing they taught us
Jody learned the first time.
They used him to show right breathing and a good kick.
The memory of that summer swishes by,
the bubbles, the blinking, the shouts,
the wonder of water holding me up
when I didn't know it would.

Now I am going to be his rescue partner,
with one of those big red float-tube things
and we are nearly all grown up.
He could ask one of those other girls
I saw him laughing with in the hallway.
He asked me.

"You don't mind getting wet, do you?" he says.
This makes me go all syrupy
and I've instantly decided to borrow
Myrtle's turquoise bathing suit
that is newer than mine.

Jody, there is a dance and we could go to it together.

During lunch Myrtle and I barely get to her house and back,
I say Hi to Peaches, her new kitten,
and her dad is there, back from rehab and quiet like before
in front of the TV,
that man needs to get a job.
He is like one of those nomads on the desert,
he wears his sweatshirt hood in the house,
he goes to rehab and comes back,
goes and comes back.
He is a night man, arranging his toy soldiers
in battles on a table when everyone's asleep.
He has 238 of them, not even four inches tall.
In the daytime he lazes in front of the TV.

I don't say anything to Myrtle about it this time,
what can I say I didn't say many times before?
On top of the TV is a new sign with Jesus' face
staring at her sleeping father,
and electric words blinking on and off: "Jesus loves you."

I meet Jody like he says at the corner of Hallway A,
and we ride two buses, way away from where we live,
to get to this pool.
Past our old school, past the blocks
where many of the shootings happen,
past the store where Jody points out
he bought his tropical fish.
I keep saying to myself the whole time,
Don'tbesojumpy. Don'tbesojumpy. Don'tbesojumpy.

I pretend to get interested in the tropical fish store.
I ask how come he is so sure
he will get out of here
and swim to college.

"You remember Victor?" he says.
Of course. I should have thought.
I nod my head. The jumpiness goes,
and in comes little Victor.
"Yeah," I said. I don't know any right thing to say,
but I think of the funniness of him when he was alive.
"His Lego-men, I can still see them
fighting, marching. Dancing."
"Well, not anymore," says Jody.
"I'm gonna get out of here."
I stay quiet, partly respecting Victor
and partly because Jody's voice shuts me out,
like he's protecting little dead Victor
from outsiders.

It must have been like the world going away
when Victor died.
It dawns on me: That's exactly when Jody's mom
must have taken him out of here.
Right then. For his sadness.
For a better neighborhood.
For a chance.

It didn't work. They're back,
she still goes to clean houses for people way early

and comes home way late. I see her
at the bus stop.

We change buses and go to where modern buildings are
and there is even a museum.
Jody has been inside it before,
he says it has paintings and sculptures in every room.
I only kept thinking how
Jody was going to see me in a bathing suit.
I was going to see him.
You know how you want something so much
and you're afraid of it too?

That pool is a dream. It's gigantic
with three diving boards, short, medium and high,
and one whole wall of glass windows,
no paint chipping or moldy smell. There is soft music
and hanging plants in the corners,
soaking up the steam and growing immense
with their privileged lives.

In the locker room
I practiced relaxing.
It didn't work.
I took those long steps out to the pool deck:
Somewhere I saw a painting once,
it was Adam and Eve,
they had such statue bodies,
growing up out of that garden they lived in,
now suddenly that painting came back to me.

Jody's little green swimming trunks
are bigger than Adam's fig leaf
but my insides feel like a window opening.
My breasts are all pointy out through Myrtle's
bright turquoise suit.
The anatomy chart in the science lab
of a man and a woman
came into my head.
Look! Don't look! said my brain.

Jody is split-second surprised with wide eyes
at the sight of me,
then his face changes,
like a tablecloth coming down over a table.
He shifts into neutral,
detaching me.
He hands me a swimming cap,
pool rules, he says,
and he gives me instructions
how to latch onto the big red rescue float tube thing
that says "Guard"
whenever it's in my reach
and says he'll save my life several different ways.
I get in the deep end and do like he says.

I am nearly inside out with jitters.
He has the float tube thing strapped across him,
he reaches it to me and I grab it
and within 3 minutes this stuff is too easy.
Jody says to start struggling
and pretend I'm drowning,

and he swims way away from me,
and then back toward me, towing the red thing
like a toy raft. I thrash around
and he disappears and next thing I know
he's behind me, hooking both arms under my arms,
hoisting my shoulders onto the red thing,
tells me to lay my head on his shoulder,
which I do and I listen while he tells me
I'll be all right.

Oh, Oh, Oh. I'll be all right,
all right. He is holding me,
kicking for both of us, saving my life
the whole length of the pool,
and I'll be all right.

We do this again and again
and I memorize my head near his neck,
his arms gripping my shoulders from underneath,
him kicking and panting
and telling me I'll be OK.

Next he tells me to really struggle,
try to grab him like I'm panicked,
the way a drowning person would get.
He goes away and swims toward me again
like before, and this time I reach out,
I get as good a hold as I can,
Oh, oh, oh, around his neck and I hang on,
and before I know it he takes me down underwater
and when I come up spluttery and coughing

he saves me the same way as before,
kicking and telling me I'll be all right.
"Jody!" I say,
and I can barely get a word out for choking,
he says, "I'm supposed to do that.
I can't save your life if I don't break your hold—"
I'm instantly a good sport again.
We do the rescues a few more times
and I think I could probably do them myself.
We rest, treading water in 9 feet
and the soft music plays and the peaceful plants grow.

"What all do you study
besides how to dunk people?" I ask him.

Jody, there is a dance and we could go to it together.

"Oh, we do injuries and CPR,"
and I can't help remembering Jolly last year,
and when I come back to the present day
I'm still looking at Jody, still treading water,
and he's saying, ". . . and the old history,
the way they used to do rescues,
here, I'll show you one. Float on your back."
I do it.
"Put your hands on my shoulders."
I do it.
"Keep your arms straight,
relax, you get a free ride."
Jody is swimming between my legs,

78

I'm not kidding.
Only rippling water between us,
I can make it romantic if I want to.

He can't read my mind. I wish he could. No, I don't.

"I can swim you miles this way," Jody says.
"Go ahead," I say. He might think I'm being a good sport
but I really mean it.

Jody, there is a dance and we could go to it together.

My mouth won't say it.
Jody swims, quietly, smoothly, steadily, looking past me,
and he says one thing. "To save somebody's life.
I'd sure like to do that."
He says it in such a heartful voice
I never heard from him before,
like he has told me a secret.
I hear myself: "Hmmmm."

I float, he swims.
"To get there in time.
And do it right. Man."
Jody is thinking about life and death,
I could not interrupt and ask him about a dance.

We stay silent, just the water lapping,
till we've gone back and forth, back and forth,
and he fastens my hands to the side of the pool

like a saving lifeguard,
and he says he has to stay and work
but I can go home now.

I stare at him.
Such a thing to say.
Is this how it is? Is this it?
Jody changes my life by touching me
and he says I can go home now.

I sulk just the least little bit, so he'll see my hurt feelings
and then I say OK.

In my room I try on the blue crushed velvet dress
I look at my legs
I do my Biology reading
and I practice grammar exercises:

Arrogance, as well as ignorance, is the foe
against which we fight.
                              Never "are the foe."
The media are embattled against the poor and the different.
                              Never "the media is."
and I get more determined.

I look up at my ceiling, and it comes into my head again:
How miserable Jody must be.
How he lost his little friend Victor
because of how the world gets so bad.
Jody must be able to see I'm parallel with him,
both of our sorry hearts

on account of my dad and Victor
both got shot to death.

But maybe he doesn't. I put my books ready
for morning
and go to bed.
Every time. Jody throws me off my balance.
And every time the balance comes back again.
In a second. A moment.
Just with the teensiest twirks of his mouth. Eyes.
He is come-here, go-away.

I think down there to him
three floors below
in an apartment just like this one.
Separated by 9 doors.
Does he wear pajamas?

LaVaughn!
Well, I just said does he or not, that's all.

24

Next morning I am more determined than ever.
I catch him going into school,
with wet hair and chlorine smell.
"Hey, Jody, I forgot to say—"
And this is a lie.
"There's that Food & Flashlight Formal,
how about going?"

Jody stops walking and looks at me
and I see his brain sizing up the question.
I want to slip down there into the concrete,
unsay what I said,
but at the same time
I am boiling with curiosity and romance.

"Sure, why not?" he says,
and I think how many days and weeks I have worried.
"Good," I say, and then I get speechless.

My first date ever.
My brain is full of that dress
and enough imagination to cover the planet.

25

"You'd be better off going to the Volleyball Volley,
we can bring a guest, you could do
your first-level bonding with the Lord,"
Annie said, same time as she handed me her shoes,
almost hanging them in the air just out of my reach.
She does not mention how she resents Jody
but the way she hangs her arm says it very clear.

"Thanks," I say. There is so much more
I want to say. I don't say any of it.
"So long, LaVaughn," she says.
"I'll take care of them," I say about the shoes.
It didn't look like I'd get another chance with Annie.
It was in her voice and readable eyes.

26

So this is how a dance feels. Music from one end to the other.
Lights turned way low and spotlights sweeping,
red, green, blue, pink, red, pink,
blue, green, red, blue, pink, green,
the cafeteria hung with balloons, shaking with sound,
even the armed guards were snapping their fingers.
Did everybody notice
Jody's gorgeousness? How could they not?

You go in and put your cans of food in the poor barrel.
Me, I didn't bring 50, I brought 3 cans of corn,
Jody brought 4 cans of tomato sauce.

There was swing dancing,
Jody knew how from his other school,
so when they played "Is You Is or Is You Ain't My Baby?"
he showed me the steps and it is
SO FUN
how the boy holds you and swings you out
and you spin and come back
and even the music shows you what to do,
you wouldn't even believe how fun it is.

Jody looked supreme
in a jacket his mom sewed over from somebody
where she cleans house.

They played "We're a Couple of Swells,"
and hundreds of us learned the words and sang it.

> We're a couple of swells, we stop at the best hotels,
> But we prefer the country, far away from the city smells.
> We're a couple of sports, the pride of the tennis courts.
> In June, July, and August,
> We look cute when we're dressed in shorts.

Nearly everybody sang, shouting out the last line
and repeating the whole thing and shouting it out again.

I danced with boys I never even saw before,
and sometimes we all just danced in a bunch,
but mostly I was next to Jody for the complete 3 hours.
I always wondered how it would feel
with a boy's arms around me.

Didn't everybody in the room
notice Jody and me?
Weren't we a beauty?
And they played "I Got It Bad and That Ain't Good,"
that song getting better with old age.
Even when there were two fights
the armed guards got them stopped right away.

How did my dress look?
Very super. My mom took special care

ironing the lace part, she loves to iron.
Except for the Pepsi that got spilled on it
my dress stayed perfect.
When they turned off all the lights
and everybody shone flashlights
you should see what a beautiful sight.
Flashing and dancing and jumping,
the beams shining around like a different kind of world,
a royal, heavenly mishmash of music and color,
Jody said how good my dress was in the bouncing light.
He said, "Look, LaVaughn, your dress,
see how it reflects double?" I was radiant.
"We're a couple of swells," we sang and laughed.

And the next part?
Well, I am getting to that.
I expected to slide right out on all that music
into swoony romance.
Jody walked to my very door with me
like a real date, we were singing "We're a couple of swells"
in these hideous terrible hallways,
and he said,
"I'm glad you made me go to the dance, LaVaughn."
I punched him on the elbow. "I did not.
I did not make you go, Jody."
"Sure you did. I mean thanks for making me go."
He looked so dreamy handsome.

"You wanted to yourself. You said."
"I mean I'm glad you decided to. It was fun."

We were agreed about that and I was jumpy as usual
and there was nothing else to say.
I had been thinking for thirteen days
what we would do next.

I took the bull by the horns.
I said, "You could kiss me, Jody."

His eyes went foreign, unexpected,
the eyelids coming down just a microscopic bit.

It was so quick it was over
before I got ready, he swooped his mouth
across me, bumping the corner of my lip
and my nose
and then he did the scariest thing,
he laughed. Little, soft. Hardly any laugh,
just a bit of a chuckle. Not even that.
And walked off down the hall.

My first kiss.
It was not a kiss.
Yes, it was.
Oh, no. It wasn't a kiss.

My bloodstream wobbled.
My mom was waiting to examine my breath and eyes
for alcohol and drugs like they say to do,
I don't know how I showed them to her with minimum words
and I got to my room and closed the door.

A big strong brave girl
would not go crying to her mirror,
"What's wrong with me?"
over and over and over
like a dodo.

A mature person
would not pretend her pillow
was Jody and kiss it
all crying wet tears all over it
even with stuff coming out her nose.

Somebody logical would not
wake in the middle of the night
and get up and go over to the chair
where the beautiful dress was draped over
and put her face down in it
to try to smell the delicious chlorine
and cry so confused
about everything being so spoiled.

Part Two

27

You want to know the worst part?
You know those little baby birds on my ceiling,
the ones I painted? Well?
If Jody and I are going to get married
and have little babies in a safe nest like that,
how can we
if I'm not good enough to kiss without laughing?

I expected to come back after the dance
and look in the mirror
and see a different face.
My own mouth transformed. A secret spell on me.

Laughing? But it wasn't a real laugh
any more than it was a real kiss.

28

Bright and early the next morning
my mom wants to know how the dance was.
In the light of day I make my face blank,
I tell her the music, the dresses, the shining flashlight beams.
She looks me up and down, checking.

I insisted down in my heart
I would not say a thing to her
about what happened
about how I cried.

There had to be somebody to tell.
Myrtle & Annie, out of the question.
Ronell? We weren't together all that long,
I didn't know where she stood on kissing and love.
I folded three cartloads of towels at the hospital
and piles of sheets for the oncology floor,
you don't want to know the illnesses these little ones have,
your heart would break.

And folding that laundry,
Jeremy and Jilly came into my mind,
the friendly souls they used to be,
those little wet ones I baby-sat last year,
and I missed them.
Jolly. I would talk to Jolly.
Even with her being back in school
to try to get some credits
we hardly run into each other.
And I feel bad not going to see Jeremy and Jilly
in Day Care.
I had my mind so much on Jody and the dance
and Myrtle & Annie
and my new class and all that homework.

The minute I called Jolly
and asked her how she's doing
with those little kids growing bigger all the time,
she needs me.

"Jolly, I know it's hard," I tell her,
"you do a real good job.
How're you doing, can I help?"
Those words were my old habit of talking to her.

"I had warning slips,
they said I had 6 but I could only find 4,
they said I been cutting school
and I ain't.
And Day Care says Jilly don't have

a right change of clothes,
hey, LaVaughn, you gotta see Jeremy can do a 'J'
for his name, you gotta hear Jilly,
she says 'potty' but she don't know to go in it.
She gets ahold of everything, she got a knife yesterday.
Where you *been?*"

I tell her, "Jolly, you got to put the knives way back
behind the faucets. You know, back where
you turn the water on?"

I went too far. She says, "You come over here and try.
See if you can do everything at the same time.
OK, LaVaaaaaaaaughn?"
She says my name in her resentful way.

"Jolly, I— I'm not trying to— Jolly?"
I don't know if she's there in the blank silence.
Then she says, "Yeah, you can help.
The reading. In the classes.
It's too hard.
The words are too big. I can't do it, LaVaughn. With these kids,
it's too much. I can't.
Here, let me read you a word they have on the assignments."
She gets off the phone and comes back
spelling words to me:
"E-x-i-g-e-n-c-y. What kind of a word is that?
And this one too: v-i-r-u-l-e-n-t.
And here too, another one: r-e-t-r-o-a-c-t-i-v-e.
How come they make me read words like that? It ain't fair."

And I agree with her.
She's got two babies, with nearly no help at all
except Day Care at school,
she's got absolutely no mom or dad anywhere,
the only foster parent she ever told me about is dead,
those boys who liked her for sex
didn't bother to notice the babies they caused,
and now she has to read those words
that would be hard for anybody with such bad education.

"I'll come over," I say.
But I get the feeling I won't be telling her my mystery
of Jody only pretend-kissing
and laughing
when I wanted to have my first real kiss ever.

And that turns out to be true.
I go to Jolly's like the bad old days of last year,
and Jeremy isn't exactly sure who I am,
and that makes me feel double bad
about getting distracted by my life
and not visiting him.
We play a game of frogs jumping on a board,
and I read a book to Jilly who is honestly cuter than before,
and I try going over Jolly's reading with her,
but she doesn't sound out a word by its parts.
I wasn't much help.
In their house there was only poor food,
flaky sugar cereal and mac & cheese in boxes.
They don't have much choice at the City Food Pantry

where they get free food once a week.
And her counters had not been washed
in who knows how long. I scrubbed and I found
a can of tuna fish to go with the mac and cheese
and Jeremy and Jilly were so cute eating
I wanted to laugh and cry both.

Going home on the #4 bus I think
how absurd:
Jolly had her whole life rearranged on her
because of boys kissing her and doing sex with her.
And I even thought about complaining to her about Jody
not giving me a passion kiss?
Not a chance.

29

I did not go anywhere near to where Jody would be
for days. I took the long way around everywhere,
not crossing his path at any time of the day or night.

I had memorized his times of leaving and coming home,
it was easy.

What was hard was the lumps
coming up a dozen times a day
in my throat. More than a dozen.

Patrick asked me, "How was the dance, LaVaughn?"
He is so slow with his words, I want to hurry him.
I said it was real fun,
not looking up.
He went on being a lab partner
still in his same two shirts.
We check our spores together,
trying to grow the haploid gametophytes.
And he showed me a shortcut to remember NADP

in photosynthesis.
He acts like everything is OK.
But he doesn't try to carry my books for me again.

30

Myrtle & Annie prayed for me
at their Volleyball Volley that same night as the dance.
"We put your name on the Miracle Hope List," Myrtle says.
"What does that list do to me?" I asked her.

Myrtle laughs her same laugh I'd know anywhere.
Her laugh is a whole memory to me
of being little together as long ago as Head Start.
Even lunch amused us. Noodles and carrots were hilarious.

"It don't do anything bad to you,
it gets you closer to the miracle," she says.

She still didn't answer my question exactly.
Would that list mean God knows who I am now?
And how do they know God is listening?

I don't understand any of it. I tell Myrtle this.
"You would if you'd join in," she says, turning away.
She doesn't ask how the dance was,

and neither does Annie, who resents it with her eyes.
I give her back her shoes and I say thanks.

After school they work on their costumes
for a play their club is having. I ask.
"It's about Noah's Ark and we're being dinosaurs,
we'll do the play for the little kids, to teach them."

I laughed. "Noah's Ark didn't have dinosaurs on it."
Annie is sudden: "How do you know? Were you there?"
"Well, no," I stay reasonable. "But they were extinct by then."

"LaVaughn, you just don't know. Listen,
God made the world in seven days,
so that means dinosaurs were on the Ark."
Myrtle & Annie *used* to know it wasn't that way.
I keep calm but I say it clear:
"Noah's Ark was way long after.
From the time the earth started, 4 billion years ago—"

"You mean thousand," says Myrtle. "It's actually 5,000."
"No, I mean billions, all those zeros go after it," I say.

"LaVaughn, you are so wrong. You need to come
to our club and find out. Don't you see?" says Annie.
The stubborn distance between us
gets bigger every day. The next thing I know
they eat lunch with their Jesus Club study group
every Tuesday and Thursday.
The Joyful Universal Church meets in a different church now
and they hunch together over the cafeteria table

arguing about their favorite club leaders,
and where is best to have club meetings.

We were together since Head Start and
I am letting them push me away, day by day.

31

On Saturday night
I watched my mom making herself too pretty,
too detailed for just a night out with those women
she takes the job stress off with once in a while.
They go to a movie, a real laugher, and they howl together,
or a real crier, and they sob together,
and they have Chinese food after,
and they make a fuss over the movie for hours,
changing the ending to make it better, or even the middle,
till I wonder why they saw it in the first place.
Once I went along. But their voices
were too drowning out for me.

But this night my mom is not just
going with those women, I could tell.
It wasn't just pants and old shoes and a jacket.
It was a dress.

My mom can really wear a dress.

Something was up.

32

My hunch was right.
It wasn't the movie women
my mom put a dress on for.

Mixed-feelings LaVaughn.
I am loyal in loving my dad my whole life long,
so is my mom too, no doubt about that.
It is 10 years since that time
when she found out he was killed
and she has been a double parent since.

Photographs of my dad are everywhere,
there's one beside the clock in my mom's room
so she sees it when she reaches to turn off the alarm.
A picture of my dad hangs in the bathroom
in a waterproof frame
never getting any older
smiling big and nice forever.
This is a mom who loved her man.

So when she puts on a dress for another man

I got nervous and upset,
wanting her to be happy
but not wanting her to be happy with a man not my dad.

33

His name is Lester.
He is at her new job, he is in charge of something there.
And he is coming to our house to eat supper.

My mom is a good cook, she brags
she never has those packages like at Jolly's house.
"Things with sauce" she calls them
and she insists, "We need sauce, I'll make sauce."
Now Lester is coming and I'll see what he looks like.

I still have my mind on Jody
and it's hard to concentrate on the rest of life
and now we get Lester. My throat goes lumpy.

My mom tells me to climb on the kitchen stool
and get down the good plates, three of them,
plus three more for dessert plus one for the rolls.
She tells me to move the stool to the other cupboard
to get the glasses we only use on holidays
when the aunts are here.

This Lester has some special stomach
to need all these special plates and holiday glasses.
Is it because he has a good job?
Is it because my mom is lonely?
I'm lonely, and I eat on the regular plates
every single time.

"Oh, and LaVaughn, you'll wear something nice, won't you?
How about that green sweater with the pretty stitching?"
I honestly believe I hear my mom cooing.
Ick.
It makes me queasy.

I sit on the stool and tear up the lettuce
wondering what will happen
and resenting dressing up for Lester
when it's Jody I dress for every day,
all the time sneaking and hiding from wherever he might be
to make sure he won't see me.

It's just a mouth.
Two mouths.
Jody's mouth and mine.
Just mouths, that's all.
Just the thought can take me out of whatever room I'm in.

34

Lester arrives in person,
he is carrying live flowers in paper.
I feel bad immediately for my grudge on him.
He leans forward, he shakes my hand, his hand is soft.

My mom exclaims so bright over the flowers
and tells me almost in a song voice
to get the blue patterned ceramic pot and put them in.
Only she says "arrange," not "put."

If Lester could read minds
he would see the history going between my mom and me.
That blue patterned pot
was a wedding gift. She always keeps it on that shelf
and it is sacred.

I reach up for the pot,
keeping my ears alert to their conversation.
I have to prop the flowers up against each other
purple and yellow and smelling fragrant.

Lester sees me drop an aspirin in the water
and crush it with a spoon, and he asks me why.
I tell him it keeps flowers fresh longer.
Lester says, "A brilliant idea, you must be a brilliant girl."

I would feel flattered
but Lester evidently doesn't get it
about how known this is about aspirin. It was in science
way back in school.

My mom says, "Oh, LaVaughn, they look so pretty,
put them in the center of the table, will you, dear?"

Listen to her. The table has a middle
but tonight it has a center.
On the table is a tablecloth my mom ironed twice.

I watch Lester trying to fit in.
He is hearty and cheerful,
he looks around the table with all the matching things
and he asks me how I like school.

I still have my unprepared attitude toward Lester.
I think about the bathroom
which my dad in the waterproof picture frame
is gone from.

I tell Lester school is fine.
Lester tells me I have a real nice mother,
he hopes I appreciate her.

"She moved into that department,
she woke them all up,
your mother is the star of the office," he says.

Lester helps me carry the dishes of food,
each dish he says, "Mmmm, it's the real thing."

I wonder what unreal food he eats on a regular basis.
The food is all set out, he pulls my mom's chair
out from the table, waits so she bends ready to sit
and then he pushes it in under her.
It is a particular motion of manners
I was not much familiar with.
We pass the dishes. My mom has truly done it up this time.
This fish with curry in the sauce is one of my favorites
and she also made some delicious potato thing.
All I did was the salad, but Lester makes sure he appreciates it
up one side and down the other,
same time as he is appreciating the fish and potatoes
and the rolls. Lester compliments "how magnificent
the vahze looks" with the flowers in it.

And candles. We have candles burning sometimes
when my mom cooks special food
or when I feel bad and need lifting up
or when she does. And on holidays for the aunts.
Tonight we have candles for Lester.

My mom tells Lester I am going to go to college.
"It was her own idea, she thought of it all by herself,

didn't you, LaVaughn?"
I agree, yes, I came home that day in 5th grade
when we saw a college movie in school.
"But it was my mom
that started my special college savings account," I tell him.
"She puts money in it from every paycheck," I tell him.
Lester says, "Well, I'm proud to know you and your mother."
This Lester is respectful to the things my mom is respectful to
and it looks like he's gonna be around.

My father's name was Guy.
I say that name in my mind while I'm eating the fish.
He would go skateboarding with Jody,
they would elbow each other, laughing.
Jody would see the real LaVaughn,
he'd kiss me in the swimming pool.
My father would tell me in the kitchen
eating cookies together
he likes Jody, he is proud I made a good choice.
It wouldn't matter so much about Myrtle & Annie.

I go to sleep that night looking up at the birds' nest,
pretending that other life I don't have.

35

Lester says eyther and nyther
in addition to vahze. I asked my mom.
"Well, Lester has high standards," she explains.

She has started plucking her eyebrows.

I'm still hiding from Jody morning and night,
wanting every day just to look at him.

My mom appreciates Lester appreciating her.
It's been a long time
anybody looked at her with value
that way.
She organized the Tenant Council for our building,
she has meetings, makes phone calls, lines up building patrols,
makes sure the self-defense classes for girls age 12 go smooth.
She hardly had time in my childish years to have some fun.

And now this Lester.
This week I didn't see her Tuesday till Thursday.
But there was good food with a note in the fridge.

"LaVaughn honey I know you like this stew and noodles and be sure you do your homework. LOVE"

It was lonely and I left the kitchen light on till morning.

36

The photographs from the dance came in,
I went to the office to pick them up.
I am amazed. It was real. Jody and I look like a magazine cover
except for my hair on one side.
We are both grinning so big.

I suddenly had the courage to take
one of the 2 copies right to him.
So what if he didn't get the kiss right?
Maybe it was his first kiss too? Maybe not. Maybe?
So what if I've been hiding ever since?
That boy in the picture looks happy.

Would I have the courage to just go ahead and use the key,
walk in the door and leave the picture there?

Yeah. I would.
The key has a dab of blue paint for identification.
I stood in front of his door, ringing the bell.
Nobody answered. I knew nobody would.

I felt like an intruder.
I put the key in the lock,
opened the door
and walked in their silent house.

Then my throat was full of heartbeat,
but I walked in braveness over to the aquarium
right on the table, I said hello to the colorful fish
with their silent, staring faces,
I propped up the photograph against the side of the tank.

I inhaled, even shaking like I was.
Over there is Jody's bedroom. Just four steps away.
I went on tiptoe, right to his door.
On the wall are underwater pictures of fish.
There is his bed
and shirts and pants. Oh. His pillow. Oh.
I took two steps in, I bent way over,
I smelled his pillow,
I never smelled a boy's pillow before.
My arm brushed the swim goggles hanging on a chair
and it gave me worse jitters than ever.

I felt like a criminal,
I hurried out so fast
before I had a chance to admit I liked it.

I taped the other photo up on my own bedroom wall
for my private enjoyment.
It is evidence,
like the songs continuing to play.

37

I get used to coming home from The Children's Hospital
and finding Lester in our house.
Some aroma comes along with him.
Aftershave or something.
Not exactly perfumy, but something.

The night when I come home and there he is
on the kitchen stool,
perched, an alarm goes off in my chest.

There's nothing wrong with Lester being there.
It's just a stool.

But it is a stool I have sat on for my whole life.
It is the stool where my mom and I have had our conversations
since I was big enough to converse with.
We have been mad there and I have cried there and she has
praised me there
and nagged me there too.
I have sat there with my mom cooking for me
since I was a child.

And before me, my own father sat on that stool
while my mother cooked for him.
And here is Lester
on the stool.
Like I said, my chest pulsed louder.

I merely said hello to my mom and to Lester too.

I got an apple from the fridge and took it to my room,
passing by the picture on the wall of Jody and me dancing,
and blowing it a private kiss
like somebody in a movie. Nobody is watching,
I can blow a kiss to anybody I want.

I sat on my bed and ate the apple.
I gave myself five minutes before starting
the homework piled in my backpack.
I laid back on my bed and looked up at the birds' nest
among the branches.
And I had so many questions to ask somebody.
Wouldn't it be perfect if you knew for sure
there was a God up there
beyond those birds?

38

I have lurked for days, weeks,
taking special effort to go around
all the back ways I can think of,
hiding from the person I want to see most.
Then with all my deafening heart beatings
I deliver his photo by hand
in person to his own personal home
and he just goes on regular
like nothing happened at all.

But four days after I propped the picture up
leaning on the fish tank in Jody's living room
this note is taped to my locker door:
"Thanks for pic. Where are you Buddy?"

My heart goes *cluuung, cluuung, cluuung*
there in the hallway. I stare.

I am constantly concerned with Jody
and his life of feelings
and he doesn't notice.

I untape the note very carefully, not to rip it,
I tuck it in my purse. I go down the hall humming
"I Got It Bad and That Ain't Good."

39

Holidays we bring the aunts to our place,
the aunts of my mom,
Aunt Verna and Aunt LaVaughn
who raised her. I got both names
and they always get a pleasure out of my growing
and making them proud like they say.
They are quite creaky of old age.

I ride the bus to where the aunts live
then bring them in a taxi
due to too many crazy people on buses.
The aunts are afraid of the crazy people.
My mom used to do this bringing
but then I got old enough.
Afterward my mom takes them home in a taxi
with the food leftovers,
while I clean up from the feast.

This year Lester offered to do the bringing
in his brother-in-law's car

but that car broke down
so it was like before: I brought the aunts.

We keep things quiet for these shriveled ladies
and we don't spice the food much.
Aunt Verna has a walker
and somebody has to go along to the bathroom
as she can't see well
and could trip on the doorboard.
And her hearing aid keeps not working.
Aunt LaVaughn has false teeth and arthritis
and she jumps when there is noise.

The aunts won't let my mom throw anything out,
even string, aluminum foil,
paper bags. The food they leave on their plates
they put back in the serving dish.
My mom doesn't try to change their ways,
they raised her from a child, she is grateful.

We are careful of them
because they are old and they are ours.
In the Great Depression
when nobody had any money in all America,
they had their childhood in that awful time.
"But it wasn't like this," says Aunt LaVaughn.
"You could walk the streets.
People waved, said hello.
Now they knock you down, rob you."
Aunt Verna says "the criminal element" twice
and shakes her head.

We get home to our house
and Jody comes in my mind, skateboarding
way across town at all hours, in danger.
I take the aunts to my room first thing,
I show them my painted tree and birds' nest.
They say, "Oh, mercy, such artistic talent,"
but also how I painted a wall I don't own.
I tell them I used the watercolor paints
they gave me for my 10th birthday.
The aunts go all smiley with pride.

Next they meet Lester.
He is very "How do you do,"
full of "how good you raised your niece,
you should be proud of the good job you done."
The aunts are not overly interested.
They do not like getting told what they should be.

My mom and the aunts go back so far,
she can sense in her sleep
if one of them has a pain or toothache.
She gets up and goes to the phone
and sure enough she sensed right.
Lester doesn't get it at all.
But he doesn't let that stop him
smiling and appreciating the aunts,
promising he knows a better kind of hearing aid battery,
he'll bring one, no, he'll bring a whole box of them.

While I was showing my ceiling to the aunts
my mom answered the phone and it was poor Jolly,

my mom asked her what was the matter
and she said their stove
all of a sudden doesn't work,
she can't cook the food they got from charity.
My mom tells Jolly to bring everybody over here
to get fed.

She whispers to me,
"Well, you tell me, LaVaughn, what would *you* do?
Now you set more places at the table—"
Her voice raises louder.
"Wait, no, you and Lester bring your desk from your room,
add it to, right over there, put a sheet over it—
And bring some piles of your books for the little ones to sit on.
And find some boxes for chairs.
And forks. Find those plastic ones."
Lester hurries to make places for everyone,
he gets stimulated by helping make do.

Now this becomes a houseful
with Jolly and Jilly and Jeremy added in,
those little ones I spent nearly a year curled up with.

But it's confusing to the aunts.
Jolly never had anybody to teach her
social manners with old people,
she says Hi to them, not anything respectful of their old age.
Aunt Verna wants to hold Jilly
but Jilly pulls on her hearing aid
and it's too much for poor old Aunt Verna.
Jeremy goes in my room and wants the dried orange from Jody

which I moved to the windowsill from my desk.
I tell Jeremy no, I almost snap at him,
then I hug him and he forgives me.
His glasses get bent behind a sofa cushion
when he takes them off to be a turtle in the living room,
but Lester straightens the earpiece again for him.

Aunt LaVaughn says to my mom
how good my art is in my room,
but also, "You shouldn't let her deface property like that."
My mom takes in a deep breath and says, "I'm doing the yams
just the way you taught me, Aunt LaVaughn,
here, smell these."
And so the subject changes.

It takes a while to gather all around to eat.
Jeremy and Jilly have not seen such a dinner table,
it's obvious looking at their big-eyed faces
and their happy reaching hands.

Lester lifts his cider glass,
he says he wants to toast my mom for her goodness
and Aunt LaVaughn pokes Aunt Verna
so she'll know what we're doing,
and everybody raises a glass or a cup,
the old aunts and even down to Jeremy
with his glasses back on
and sitting up proud on the kitchen stool.

Jilly is on my lap playing with my napkin
but she helps me lift my glass

and we toast my mom. Like Lester says, "her good heart
and cooking." He's excited about having an audience.

My mom is somewhat frowzyhaired
from the many messes we had—
1 was the gravy splattered
when Lester poured it out of the pan,
2 was trying to find enough chairs
and inventing some from boxes,
Jilly and I are on a box.
3 was Jilly pulled on the tablecloth and I caught her
just before the whole arranged table capsized,
and 4 was the spilled cranberry sauce all across the kitchen
when Aunt LaVaughn insisted she could carry it to the table.
There were other messes, too, but here was dinner,
smelling good, in many colors, and hot.

You could say Jody kept interrupting
even though he didn't set foot in the room.
We are passing the turkey, he comes to my mind,
how smooth and strong his arms are. He goes away again,
I ask Aunt Verna which part she'd like me to serve her.

My mom finds Jolly's napkin on the floor,
puts it back on her lap,
Jody's eyes come to my imagination,
and I'm distracted too much by them.
To tell the truth, my heart wasn't in the feast
like it used to be,
not with Jody living 3 floors below
in the same floor plan.

Lester keeps putting himself in
where this was always the aunts' dinner in years gone by.
These aunts knew what my dad looked like,
how his voice was,
how he walked into a room.
Here's Lester, talking about a gadget
he's going to buy from TV where he saw it,
it's the best invention ever made,
it will fix every hinge, every cupboard door,
and nobody is listening.
The only one noticing him
is Jeremy, staring from across the table,
his eyes so wide behind his glasses
and a piece of turkey breast in his hand,
paused in the air.

I make a mental count: Everybody here
wouldn't have a place to go today
if it wasn't for my mom.
She isn't easy to have for a mom,
she has too many opinions for one family,
she can make me want to slam doors and stick out my tongue
but I don't do it because of the long run.
That's my mom
with her small working wage,
feeding 6 people that wouldn't have anywhere to go.

40

I carry Jody's note everywhere
tucked in with my student ID,
as a good luck charm.
The Science Aptitude Test has me so scared,
the teacher said it's so important,
and Patrick is studying hard for it every night, even at work.
He memorizes data while he slides burgers across a counter.
This test is for Placement, another word I didn't know about.
They see what score you made and if you scored high
they give you harder classes.
On his notebook page
Patrick draws a little guy with whirly question marks
all around him
and we look up "endoplasmic reticulum" again.

That Biology class is the quietest place.
Everybody pays attention, nobody knocks over microscopes,
people ask their questions one at a time,
there are enough books for everybody to have one,
and our fern spores and stained slides
are there the next day when we need them.

And nobody is sleeping anything off
with their heads hanging down
in this hidden-away class
that I never would have found all by myself.

Ronell took the Science Aptitude Test last year
and she says she had nightmares
but the adrenaline rush was worth it,
and it got her into a computer class she wanted.
A test being so important I wouldn't sleep through the night
was a surprise to me. I never had that before.
Over and over I woke up
with the streetlight shining on my ceiling tree.
I would think over how every eggplant is female,
about platyhelminthes and sporangia and hydrogen bonding.
Then comes a bang and the streetlight went out.
Somebody out there with a gun again. I jump every time.
Like always, my mom is in my room
before the sirens start.
She checks if I'm OK, she puts her arms around me.
It is so scary if I let myself think about it.
So I think about getting out of here instead.

I wonder if Jody jumped out of sleep in his bed
three floors below when the gunshot happened.
It must bring back Victor every time.
Those two little boys, I guess they loved each other.

The next day I get out of three classes
to go way over to another high school to take
the Science Aptitude Test

along with people I never saw before.
It was hard, with words I never saw,
and questions longer than I ever read before,
about semiconductors, warming oceans, melting glaciers,
migration of tropical diseases,
And many answers looking as right as each other.

Frankly I can see why so many people
say they'll never study a thing
ever again after high school.

And that thought stops me in my tracks:
I am going to college
and I am going to live in a place
where you hear something besides gunshots and sirens,
where green grass grows.

And I try so hard on the Science Aptitude Test,
I am dizzy by the end,
my brain is cooked with so many facts and evidences.

Patrick and I sit together on the bus back to school.
We don't talk about the test.
Patrick asks me what I do when I'm not in Biology.
I tell him I go up to the hospital and fold laundry.
Patrick points to the "Jody Jody Jody"
printed all over my notebooks. "Which Jody is that?"

Hearing somebody else say that name out loud is jolting.
I say, "Oh, a friend of mine."
My voice refuses to get controlled.

"Jody with the tattoos, or Jody with the leather?" he says.
"No, Jody with the skateboard," I say.
"Oh," says Patrick. He looks at me steadily.
"Well?" I say. I don't want him staring.
"Then it's not your boyfriend," Patrick says.
I don't say anything. I look out the window.
He's not being fair,
he shouldn't corner me like that,
asking about my private life.

I ought to like Patrick more than I do.
I guess he has just those two shirts.
Instead I concentrate on Jody:
I wonder if he and I could be in the same college
or if my score on the test will make me
never go to college at all.
It's none of Patrick's business
that Jody isn't my boyfriend yet.

41

Myrtle & Annie were practicing another play, and
it was a chance to get back my lost place, so I went.
They drew me a map to get there,
this is the third church where their club has set up.

There was a loud band of drums, guitar and keyboards.
Seven kids, big and little, carried in a long sign
and hung it above the stage:
"Iniquity or Heaven? It's Your Choice"
and everyone clapped and cheered for the sign
so I clapped too. I wasn't sure of "iniquity."

Bright-colored spotlights started moving around
and the band got louder.
I could see the club members had worked hard
on their costumes. And they also had large labels
saying which sins they were.
One girl was a heroin needle with a big long spike on her head.
One was unmarried sex, dressed in prostitute clothes.
One person was a gang knife of shiny foil
    with red painted blood.

One was a cigarette
and one very tall boy was a whiskey bottle.
One person was abortion; I needed to see the label for that
because she had on a plastic bag
splotched with red paper for blood spurts.
One person was a gun
and one was a homosexual,
a boy wearing lipstick and a dress.

Myrtle & Annie were in the chorus
of saved people, dressed as choir singers.
Each time Jesus in his long gown
sat down on one of the sins
it crumpled up and died
and the band played and the chorus sang:

> Satan's all around you,
> Satan's law is sin.
> Heaven's waiting for you,
> Jesus lets you in.
> Jesus loves you, loves you,
> loves you, loves you, loves you.

At the end of the play
the chorus of singers
each pulled a cord at their shoulders
and wire wings came up out of the back of their robes
and they were angels
singing a sad song
about all the sinners who had to go down to Hell
and miss the fun of God's love.

131

Then Jesus and all the sinners bowed
and everyone had cake and punch
with much laughing and excitement.
Their adults congratulated them,
and put out a sign-up clipboard for joining
but I didn't write my name.

I clapped long and loud for the play,
but what could I say to Myrtle & Annie?
Their play didn't make me want to join their club.
I don't want their club telling me what to hate.
I wondered why Jesus would destroy people like that.
I walked home by myself and it kept nagging me:
What was different about us now?
Where was it that we changed?

Watching a kitten dash out of an alley
with its big ignorant eyes afraid of the street,
it came to me: Words I never even thought of before.
We used to be pure souls. Little girls
not troubled with what was a sin and what wasn't.
We had our dolls and our sadnesses
and we woke up in the mornings looking forward
to things.
Our childish lives seemed so ordinary.
They were not ordinary.
Now, walking along in the slight rain that afternoon
I felt so bad for those little pure souls,
completely changed away from themselves.

42

Myrtle & Annie and I have been Valentining
with candy hearts since we were so little
our moms did it for us.
We always know each other's locker combinations,
and we sneak around
planting candy hearts and not getting seen.
Every year it works.

But this year my heart was so worried:
Would they forget me or skip me?
Like years before, I bagged up the candies,
put red ribbons on them and a lollipop each,
trying to be first like always.
It felt like a forlorn hope,
leaving the little DEAR ONE and U R NICE and
BE TRUE candies in their lockers.
Their locker doors have stickers: "Get right with the Lord."
I wondered if they'd just give each other a look
and ignore my Valentine bags.

But when I opened my own locker,
there they were: glued down on cardboard

in the shape of a big L V,
32 candy hearts they used this time,
every one of them said EZ 2 LOVE.
My heart got bright with happiness.
Myrtle & Annie, my old friends.

The thought of Jody giving me a Valentine
kept me holding my breath.
Taking my chance while the hall
was crowded body to body
I pushed through the air vents in his locker door
the twenty candy hearts I had saved out,
all saying WHY NOT on them,
I heard them drop and scatter,
those unpunctuated hearts asking him
what I wanted to know.

When I got to Biology
there on my lab stool
was an envelope with "LaVaughn" on it,
My heart jumped. But
it was only Patrick's writing, I knew its shape by now.
The card was hand printed with all different colored markers:

> I think YOUR DNA is FUN
> I like the LAB REPORTS we make
> LAVAUGHN give me a little BREAK
> VALANTINE tell me I'm the ONE

I knew I should be nice. But I laughed,
it was so funny with those big letters and misspelling,

like a little boy would do.
I said thanks and gave him a bunch of candy hearts
I had left over in my pocket.
We chewed them and worked on cellular processes
and I tried being grateful.

The part about DNA in the book shows
how we are always the same person forever.
It's in our cells.
That means
my dad would recognize me now,
I mean our cells would recognize each other.
The huge lump comes in my throat,
I try to keep my head down till it goes away.
Patrick hands me a candy heart,
I put it in my mouth to try to dissolve the lump.
Whatever the little heart says
I don't care.

No Valentine from Jody.
Coming home from the hospital
I smelled his chlorine
and I hum "We're a couple of swells."

What did Patrick mean,
"Then it's not your boyfriend"?

Part Three

43

Next thing I know Lester is telling my mom
where a house is going up for sale
by the cousin of somebody he knows from a job he had once
and it would be a perfect home for the three of us.

In my room, doing my homework
with my door not completely closed
I perk up my ears. Leave Jody!
Two days after Valentine's Day he let me try
his skateboard. It wasn't as hard
as I thought, he didn't laugh at me,
he even caught me when I started to fall.
He didn't mention the candy hearts
scattered in his locker. Does that mean
he guesses it's somebody else entirely?

If I could say to him, "Jody,
I was the one who sprinkled all those hearts in there."
But I can't.

Leave Jody!

We have always lived in this plain place.
Here is where my mom and dad came when they had me,
it was not such a slum then.
My dad walked in these rooms
holding me when I was a crying infant,
and I always say I want to get out of here.
But not yet.
We would be living where my dad never was.

I hear my mom digging her heels in,
refusing to get excited too fast,
knowing in her smart way
nothing is as good as the advertising says.

Leave Jody!

Lester tells this distant house like a story.
"There's carpet every inch of the home,
and paneling, and the windows are set like this, see,
the stove, the fridge, and right there are the cupboards,
I can see you in that kitchen,
happy as you can be."

My mom's voice rings out:
"And there's a room for LaVaughn?"
"Oh, sure," says Lester. "A real nice room for her.
I wouldn't even consider it if it didn't have a room for her."

Lester goes on about the porch, the tree in the yard.
Leave Jody!
And what about school? And Myrtle & Annie?

140

I can't just go out of my room and say it,
but by this time I'm over near the door,
my ear to the gap, listening to Lester's promises.
"Oh, the schools there are the best.
Every child gets an excellent education."

And there are Ronell and Doug and Artrille,
the Brain Cells and the grammar hats,
we have to learn whole lists of words:
"disparate," "vigilance," "anguish," "trajectory,"
"fallible," "grotesque," "insight," "disheveled," "inert,"
"aspiration and lassitude," "energize and enervate."
Dr. Rose says, "We rely on clichés, we become clichés.
We must not be   ensnared
by   our   imagined   limitations."

And Biology with Patrick,
where we just learned yesterday that protons are everywhere
and decay is essential to life.
Now, learning this might not make everybody jump for joy,
but it sure helps me begin to make sense of how the world is.

And we'd live far away from the aunts
and The Children's Hospital.
This is my future Lester is talking about.
They don't decide it right away.
But he calls often late at night, waking me with the ring,
wanting my mom to remind him she likes him.
I hear her side:
"Sure. Sure I do. Yes, sure. It's late, Lester, I have to work
tomorrow. I know, Lester. Yes, sure I do. Lester, I'll see you

when we said. Friday. I was already asleep. Goodnight, Lester.
Sure. Sure I do. Goodnight, Lester. Yes, sure I do. Goodnight."

And once it was to tell her how many square feet
of counter
the kitchen has.

44

Will my mom marry Lester and move us away?
She has been my two parents for all this long, long time.

And she is deserving.
Lots of other moms marry new husbands all the time.
I tell Myrtle & Annie. They go sad in their eyes,
and I feel better for a whole day.
They say they'll pray for me.
"You mean you'll pray for me
not to have to move away?" I ask, and
Annie says, "We pray for God's will to be done."
"And what's God's will?" I ask her.
"Only God knows that," she says.

But I don't get it. If God's will gets done anyway
because it is God's will,
what's to pray for? And is all the horribleness
of the world God's will?
How come?

And what did Patrick mean,
"Then it's not your boyfriend"?

45

I'd hate to leave The Children's Hospital.
One little girl on the oncology floor
needs a bone marrow transplant,
she's been waiting and waiting.
We saw each other when I delivered the sheets.

She looked up at me, this ill child with a crooked-teeth smile
and my heart went right from my chest to her bed
and I went along after it and picked up the book she had there
and I read it to her.
Then I ended up making finger puppets of two washcloths
and her name is Lee Anne
and that such a child
should have such an illness—there is no justice
in this mad world of cruelty.

And besides. The ones with no hair from treatment,
there is one with no feet from birth.
Maybe I could be a nurse or somebody
to help these little ones.
I wonder what you have to do to learn how to be a nurse.

In my laundry job I help but not much.
I left work that night hurting about Jody, Lee Anne,
and leaving everything behind.

46

The house Lester is hankering for
and is waiting for the price to go down,
my mom and I eat supper about it,
we clean the house about it,
we discuss it in the kitchen
without our stool which Lester has disappeared with
to repair it where he loosened the legs
by sitting on it with his body size.

I try to be reasonable, I try to be a good sport,
I mention leaving Myrtle & Annie, Biology,
I mention the Brain Cells,
I bring up the hospital and Lee Anne.
I don't dare mention Jody
because I can't say his name and keep my voice regular.
It will be a safer neighborhood and a yard too, she says.
I ask her if she has seen this yard and neighborhood.
Well, no, not yet.
She's going out there with Lester this weekend.
She says There's no metal detectors at the school over there.
And I think how she should say "There are no metal detectors."

"Wouldn't you like a yard, some flowers?" she asks me.
I think how Lester's flowers are the only ones she's seen
up close in many a year.

I say, "Well, a yard would be nice."
She accuses me of having the voice of a teenager.
I ask her what voice she wants me to have.
"Verna LaVaughn, you watch your mouth," she says.
I do it instantly.

The bargain is: I watch my mouth, she gives me
the life I get, a roof over my head
like many in the world don't have. It's not the
most comfortable bargain, but it is what we have.

Lester comes here again with flowers. They go in
my father's wedding pot. Tonight we have shrimp
in a creamy sauce with green things in it.
Lester says, "Mmm, this is the real thing,"
and he pushes my mom's chair in under her at the table,
and he reminds me how I need to appreciate my mom.
Something about the way Lester says "appreciate."
It has a tone of voice.

I mention leaving my room behind and its birds' nest.
"There's real birds out there, real nests, the real thing,"
says Lester. His voice chimes in some way.

After supper I do homework and think about Jody.
I hardly hear my mom and Lester talking beyond the door,
even though I leave it open just a breath.

But something clicked.
I was leaning my head on the wall memorizing science
and a little button in my mind clicked.
Lester was saying, "And you don't get hassled about the rent."
My mom says, "Hassled?
Why would anybody hassle you about rent?"

"Well," Lester says. "You know. How they are."
My mom says no, she doesn't know how they are.
I hear my mom loud and clear:
"Lester, nobody hassles you for rent if you pay it on time.
I have never been hassled for rent in all the years."
Then Lester says something I don't hear clearly.
My mom says, "A landlord asking for rent is not hassling.
That's not hassling, Lester."

Again Lester says something soft,
they laugh together, the refrigerator door opens,
dishes move on shelves, the door closes again,
I return to my homework.

But Jody swims up in front of the coelenterates
as he does so often,
splush-splush-splushing the water with his arms,
looking past me with his wondrous eyes,
swimming between my legs.
My heart floats.

47

I still have Jody's note with me at all times
and here he is in the elevator one night, in person,
after the hospital. Outside the wind is blowing so hard
everybody is relieved just to be in the filthy elevator
with all the bad words written on its walls.
"Hey, LaVaughn, where you been?" he says.
My heart shoves me to tell him everything.
I tell him nothing.

"Oh, I don't know," I say. "We might be moving," I blurt.
Did I expect him to be sad,
get down on his knees with love, beg me to stay?
He says, "Whoa, LaVaughn. This place won't be the same."
Don't you even care, Jody?
Doesn't it even make any difference?
I've smelled your pillow in your very own bedroom.
"Where?" he says. One little word, simple curiosity.
"I don't know, some kind of house. With a yard."

His eyes catch on. A yard
is a meaning all by itself, a thing people pray for.

"I'll miss you, LaVaughn," he says,
and he gets out at his floor.
Does this make things better or worse?

I'm so rattled up inside I don't even know.

48

Today Dr. Rose gave us our lies and lays.
Like other grammars, this one took the room by surprise.
You never just lay down on your bed
unless it was yesterday or some time past.
You lay a book down on your bed
but you all by yourself lie on it.

I have always been wrong. For 15 years.
Laid is what you did with an egg
if you are a hen.
There are lains, too.
These are what you have done in the past.
I have lain on my bed with my arms around my pillow
imagining it's Jody.

Wearing our hats, we Brain Cells keep on practicing.
Doug said, "We have lain on the sidewalk bleeding
till the ambulance came for him and me."
Ronell says, "Your responsibility for learning
to talk right lies on you." And Artrille says:
"The little kids lying in The Children's Hospital

could wish their whole lives to have the strength
to do pronouns and verbs and predicates,
and they'll still lie there sick till the day they die."

I say to him, "Hey, I work there. You been there?"
Dr. Rose appears over my shoulder.
"You've been there?" she corrects me. I say it right.
"Yeah, I work there," he says.
"Doing what?" I ask.
"Janitorial, I've never lain down on the job," he says,
and he tips his hard hat in pride of himself.
I tell him I'm in laundry, and he says janitorial
is as close as he can get to doctoring right now.
"You—a doctor?" says Ronell,
and Artrille says, "Yeah, me—a doctor." He is not kidding.

We take this in.
Artrille is no richer than us. He lives in a slum like us.
He would be valuable in a gang, he memorizes things well,
he has quick eyes, they could scare you in a dark alley.
And he's strong. He can lift Ronell with one hand.
Artrille a doctor.
Doug says to him, "How you going to do that?"
Dr. Rose eyeballs him from where she is nearby.
"How are you going to do that?" Doug adds the verb in there.
And from what Artrille replied
I got encouraged for my life too.
He said, "I have never not worked since fourth grade.
I always have a job, sometimes two. I can do it."
Even my feet got excited.

Here's this plain American boy
in a poor school in a poor place
in an ugly time of people dying from guns and drugs and cruelty.

And we began calling Artrille "Doc."
The Brain Cells, four people in hats
saying right grammar in a room
that seemed like the only room where it mattered.

It was just a short conversation
but it improved the state of my mind.

Before we left that day
Dr. Rose made everyone in the room recite together:
"We will rise to the occasion,
which is life."
She made us do it twice
like a choir.

49

Myrtle & Annie shocked my system:
They decided not to come to my house
for Myrtle's birthday sleepover
which we had for seven years till now.

Instead their club had a Birthday Fest
for everybody with birthdays this month
and they played their Heavenly Host computer game.
They meet in a different place now,
this makes church number four.
My worst fears about them
were coming true.
I have known Myrtle & Annie since my father was alive.
They were with me in the blur of horribleness,
little girls in dresses at his funeral,
my life story is full of Myrtle & Annie,
as steady as daily food.

I can see us holding hands on the ice
when we believed we were skating princesses,

when Myrtle's dad took us to the rink
way long before he went to rehab.
We used to invent jump rope rhymes and jacks contests
and we made little tiny beds for our little tiny dolls,
dolls that could fit in our pockets.
They loved the triangle way my mom cut sandwiches.
We learned how to make a chocolate birthday cake at my house
and we have made it ever since.
We always hugged each other when the bad things happened:
Annie's divorces. Myrtle's father.
Our tough mothers when they wouldn't let us do things.

The birthday sleepovers were a tradition.
Now it's just Jesus. Annie doesn't have me
part her hair anymore, she has a "Heaven's For Me" headband.

"What do you get out of that club, anyway?"
I ask, I am so hurt.
Myrtle gets a whole different look on her face,
I have seen it only a few times. "We get the Lord,
we gave our life to him." It's a new voice she has.
She could be talking from a distant room.

Then Annie says, "They picked me for their
Chain of Faith." "Huh?" I say.
I am saying this more and more
to Myrtle & Annie.
"I wouldn't have to go to school,
I'd be a Chain of Faith Disciple,
I'd be bringing people to the Lord.

They'd get me my GED and I'll get paid,
they say I got what it takes to be in the Chain of Faith."

Now Annie has never liked school very much,
school subjects are hard for her
and she has nearly flunked things,
but quitting school is crazy.
Myrtle says to her, "Annie, you really don't want to do that,"
and I say too, "You really don't want to do that,"
and Annie says to me, nearly nasty,
"You don't know anything about it, LaVaughn."
And then she's sorry. She says,
"You liked the play, I saw you liking it.
Just come to one meeting.
LaVaughn?" She tilts her head down in her lifelong way,
she's been doing it since I can remember,
her eyes coding to me that she'll like me if I do what she wants.

"I don't think so," I say and I walk away,
full of rejection and pitiful sadness,
knowing I did a mean thing
and going right ahead and doing it.

50

Well, listen to this: There is a pink jellyfish
so beautiful
no human could make anything
so filmy and graceful and alive, floating along in a hidden lake
thousands of miles away from this ugly place.
There's hardly any food, so it grows
a whole garden of plants inside itself
to feed on. This jellyfish stays in the sunlight all day
and photosynthesis makes its plants green.
Then at night it goes down deep in the water
where lots of nitrogen is,
for fertilizer.
This creature
is just a jellyfish.
And it's figured out a way to go on living
when the odds are against it.

It's adaptation, I learned it in Biology,
and I keep thinking how it's a good lesson
to keep remembering.

51

Two days before another Biology test,
I had somebody's extra shift at the hospital the day before,
I wasn't getting enough sleep,
I kept having gym with Myrtle & Annie barely saying hi,
and feeling so guilty and bad about them,
watching them so cozy with their club friends,
and I was reading my Biology on the bus home.
When I got off, so did two little tiny kids,
too young to ride the bus alone,
bewildered. Maybe seven years old. Maybe eight.
"This ain't the right stop," says one,
and the other one begins to panic and cry.
I got down there in their faces,
I looked in their coats for their name tags,
laying down my Biology book on the sidewalk,
and I gave them all the tissues I had,
for they were both bawling by now something pathetic.
They were trying to go to their grandmother's,
and I was mad at her for making them go on a bus alone,

and I see the address they're carrying. It's not far.
These children are too young, they can hardly read.
By now the bus is gone.

We get on the next one together,
the familiar driver knows me
and I explain the three of us are entitled to this ride free
because these little ones made a mistake.
The driver waves us onto the bus
and we settle into a seat
and I mop up their tears some more.

I tell them a story about elephants and their families,
all how they love their babies and teach them things,
and I make up some parts about how they play together,
I entertain them all the way to their bus stop,
and there is their grandmother, they jump up when they see her
who by now I don't even like.

I tell her they got off at the wrong stop
and needed somebody to bring them to the right one.
She says I am an angel from heaven to help these little ones.
I say I am no angel from anywhere
and she ought to take better care of them.
"I said I'd be at the stop, and here I am," she says,
she is insulted by me.
I tell her, "They could be lost forever,
don't you *know* that?"
She hugs them close and walks away with them.
They wave bye-bye to me and I get myself home.

It's true about elephants,
how they love their families,
they mourn the bones of their dead.

The extra bus trip only took a half hour
but it made me mad and even more tired.
I go home and my mom is gone to a meeting,
I take three bites of leftovers
and throw myself on the bed, I leave the light on,
and I'm out.

Next thing I know
is like a dream from dreamland and I would not believe it awake.
Standing over me saying "Sleeping Beauty" is Jody
in my own bedroom like magic.

"Hey, Sleeping Beauty, here's your Biology book
you left at the bus stop."
Coming up into awakeness
my heart is too unruly to contain.
By now Jody is staring straight up
at the birds on my ceiling.
I see up his actual throat and chin from down where I am.
He plunks the book on my stomach
and continues staring.
"I never knew you had this ceiling," he says,
looking down at me with his perfect eyes.
"Who painted it?"
I tell him I did. Only in my wildest dreams would he be
here in my bedroom, and he is here in my bedroom
and I am wide awake.

"You did it like Michelangelo, LaVaughn. That's real good,"
he says. "That branch, with the knothole and all those leaves.
And birds too.
You never told me."

I had no time to remember words to say.
"You never asked," I tell him.
Jody is in my very own bedroom.

"Why'd you leave your book at the bus stop?" he says.
"How'd you get in here?" I asked him.
"I used my key, Buddy."
"Oh. The bus stop. Right.
It was some little kids. It's a long story."

Jody turned around, toward the door.
"I'll miss you, LaVaughn," he says.
"Go back to sleep, see you later."
And he left.
The click was so loud.
Then he poked his head back in.
"Clean your room, girl," he said and he was gone.

My room was full of the bright heat of Jody being there.
I did not clean one single speck of it.

52

Jolly suddenly grabs me
on my way to a Biology test,
I don't have time
to hear her emergency news right then
and her eyes go hurt.
I haven't seen her in weeks.
I promise her I'll meet her at Day Care, picking up the kids
after school,
and in the way she looks at me for just that moment
I can't even imagine her total of broken promises
already in her 18 years of life on Earth.
"I mean it," I tell her, and I give her a hug around our books.
She feels so fragile, I hold on to her an extra second
to make her know I'll be there.

The Biology test is scary, but Patrick and I
use our lab notes just right for our team answers,
I spelled the words Patrick can't spell,
And I got to explain that jellyfish.

When I get to Day Care Jeremy jumps up and down at me
and Jilly calls me my old familiar name, Bon. She's so chummy,
this child who barely escaped with her life that time.
We get her bundled up and settled in the stoller,
Jeremy alongside in his little hat,
holding my hand with his little mitten in the cold, blowing air.
Jolly begins her urgent news. She's frantic.
I listen closely from my guilt
about not paying attention lately.

It's Ricky. He is divine, the best guy ever made anywhere,
he is so cute you could die looking at him,
he appeared like magic
suddenly
and he loves the kids
and he has personally taught Jeremy to read.
Now I can't help my eyes going funny about that.
Jeremy's not yet four.

"He can too read! His name, 'Pepsi,' 'street,' 'Ford,'
he can read everything!" Jolly's breathless
about Ricky, this wonder of the world.
"He's so good with the kids,
he loves them like they're his own. . . ." She's glowing
and I'm jealous, even though it's crazy to be jealous of Jolly.

"Slow down, Jolly, start from the start," I tell her,
while Jeremy is bouncing on one foot
instead of walking straight,
yanking my hand with every step, it feels so nice.

But Jolly's life doesn't have an actual start. It goes
more in pops and lurches.

"He already got my name tattooed."
"Huh?" I hear myself so sudden. "On your what?"
We have reached the bus stop
and I hoist Jilly out of the stroller
and collapse the wheels to lift it on the bus.
Jeremy bounces, counting "sebenteen, elebentween."
"No, on him. On his shoulder. It says 'Jolly'
with a heart there. Inside the heart is where 'Jolly' is wrote."
She's gripping her books with her chin
to point to the correct place where it would be on her arm.

"Oh," I say. "That's how Jeremy learned to read?
From the tattoo?"

"You ain't listening. He teaches Jeremy.
Oh, he's so cute,
he don't get mad at the kids—
wait'll you see him."

The bus comes,
the same one I took so many times last year to Jolly's.
We sort out the kids to load them on,
clanking the stroller up the steps
and I'm thinking she does this
all by herself
every day. Through my mind goes
my personal information about Jolly:

She had a baby when she was fourteen.
Both kids' fathers have never been heard from since.
Now there is this Ricky, appearing like magic.
I can't help it, my doubts come right up to the surface
on this one.

"That's really nice, Jolly," I tell her while we get seated,
with all these pounds of heavy kids
bumping into people on every side. Jilly is on Jolly's lap,
Jeremy on mine. He puts his mittens in my hand.
I notice how he doesn't fuss with his glasses
and Jolly pulls a book from his pack and puts it in his lap
while she's talking to me.
He opens it and says, "Kittens. You read this book, LaBon."

Here is the surprise:
Jeremy says the cats are in the kitchen.
But plainly in the picture they're in the yard.
I say, "See, Jeremy, that's their yard, with trees all over."
"No." Jeremy puts his finger
on the word "kitten" and says "kitchen."

My eyes bug out.
This child is almost reading.
"Jeremy, how old are you?" I ask.
He holds up three fingers.
"How old is Jilly?"
He holds up one finger. "But near 2," he says.
Jilly is patting my hand with impatience
to get on with the story

and Jolly pokes my arm. "See?" she says.
We make wondering faces at each other
and I go on reading.
Jeremy reads with me, "pie" for the kittens' snack.

All I can say is I've got to meet this Ricky.

Isn't it so strange how life goes? So terribly, terribly strange?

53

My mom and Lester went to see the famous house.
She reports back. "It sure does have a tree in the yard.
The school is right near the house,
there hasn't been any shootings at that school.
Wouldn't you like to go to a safe school like that?
We could plant some grass where it's all caked and muddy,
the house needs a new roof,
but all houses need new roofs sometime. . . ."
I watch her undecided face.
"Well, three of the windows are broke,
but that's easy to fix." I hear my mind hearing her grammar.
Did I not ever notice it before?

"And it needs a new furnace.
And paint. And, well, insulation too.
It sure would be better for Lester,
that place he lives is a mess."

I don't say anything.
"Well? LaVaughn? The school situation?"
I don't say anything.

"What about them shootings at school?"
Those shootings. And we haven't had one lately.

"You speak when you're spoken to, Verna LaVaughn,"
and so I do.
"It's my friends and my classes,
and my job," I say.
It's the truth and yet
I don't expect her to trust my judgment.
Leave Jody! He said he'll miss me,
that's reason enough.

Even though Myrtle & Annie are completlely in their club
they are still Myrtle & Annie.
"These are friends I've had for my whole life," I remind her.
"Then they won't stop being your friends," she says.
I can't say Jody's name or she'll hear my heart.

My mom says, not to anybody, really to the window,
"It's all mud out there.
But it would be our mud."
She lets her breath out hard and puts a spoon in the sink.

So the house and the tree and the safe school and Lester
are still not sure.
I hear my mom getting up in the middle of the night,
trying to decide. Opening the refrigerator.
Moving things around on shelves.
Making tea.
Flipping magazine pages.
Turning on the TV. Turning it off.
Hmmmming in the dark.

54

There was another shooting at school today.
We hadn't had one since last year. Sirens,
ambulance, fear in everybody's eyes, even the surly ones
trying to look unafraid. I was late to one class
running around making sure Jody was still alive.
The teacher didn't notice me,
there was too much chaos and hubbub
for hours.
Our school doesn't close every time a gun goes off
the way good schools do,
but it takes a long time for everybody's heart to slow down.

And every time it happens
they try to take away the funding for Grammar Build-Up,
to hire more security guards.
It was Ronell who told me
and Dr. Rose said she was right.
"This is one reason why it is crucial
that everyone in this room,"
she looks around in her usual way
like a queen surveying her garden,
"persevere, in order to improve your grades

in all your classes." She lets this subjunctive grammar
sink down in.

"You see, your progress is being tracked
meticulously. Meticulously.
Some of you may have noticed already."
Two people raise their hands and tell
how Guidance took them in for conferences
and asked them questions
about their past and future,
all because they're in this tutorial.

"It's simple, really," Dr. Rose explains.
"If your grades show measurable improvement,
the younger ones coming along behind you will enjoy
the privilege of taking Grammar Build-Up."
She allows us three seconds to laugh if we want to.
We are too jittery from the shooting to laugh.
"If not, not.
Our funding will disappear, and, yes,
it will doubtless be used to hire
additional security guards. Ours is a dangerous world,
it goes without saying. What we need
to believe in—
to believe in thoroughly—
is that you and you and you,"
she goes all over the room with her educated eyes,
"can stand up tall, shatter those statistics
about students in the 'poorer schools,' as they call us,
and make a difference in the vast
and terrifying and magnificent world."

She is on a parade of her beliefs.
"You might not all see a specifically proportionate rise
in your grades as a result of your work
on these afternoons.
What we can demonstrate much more clearly is
your increased ability to sustain a thought."
She stares among us;
sometimes I almost feel like ducking,
it is like having an airplane aiming at your face.

"Remember, our goal is lucidity.
Gleaming lucidity.
Only when we are lucid can we be constructive.
Only when we are constructive
can we live with good conscience in the world.
Only when we live with good conscience in the world
will the rage of the people calm.

"How many of you in this room really want to go to college?
Really want to?"
All 11 of us that are left in the class raise our hands.
Doc has specially inspired our group of Brain Cells
to keep on thinking so.

"Then gather close, and listen carefully.
You might—you might—get into college
without Grammar Build-Up. But staying in.
Ah, that is the difference.
How many of our streets are littered with disappointed people
who once set foot in a college
but who could not figure out

how to make it all make sense?
We have only a few more weeks left.
A few more of these lovely afternoons.
How many of you will be here at the end?"

The Brain Cells raise our hands. And the other seven.
Somehow this strange person brings out
a pride I didn't know I had.
She says, "We will rise to the occasion,"
and we say all together back to her, "which is life."

"Very well, then. Today is 'whom.' How many of you
have ever used this word?" Three hands go up,
none in my group. But we learn this new required thing
as we have learned the others
and we don't even roll our eyes anymore.
"Someone shot a gun at school; it was grotesque."
"Whom did he shoot?"
"I don't know, but I saw the trajectory of the bullet."
"You did not. You and your fallible vigilance were in math."
"Whom else do you know who was even on the same floor?"

I can't stop wondering where Jody was when it happened.

In Biology there are chromosomal aberrations,
in Grammar there are "whom" and statistics to shatter,
at the hospital there are children who are going to die,
in school someone shoots a gun.
I don't know. I just don't know.

55

Jody and I get home at the same time.
It's pouring icy cold rain, everything drips,
we meet in the gloomy light. My skin flashes.
He says, "It could've been you, the gunshot."
"I know," I say.
He says, "I'm glad it wasn't,"
my heart goes balloony.
"I ran to see if you were alive," I tell him.
"You did?" He lets me in,
his eyes and mouth go alert.
"I did." In half a second
I'll have my arms around him,
I'll burst into fire,
he'll instantly understand,
his heart will explain it to him.
The quiet between us almost lifts my feet
to take those steps. But his eyes shift
and he's an island again
miles away,
and my feet don't move.

We get in the elevator with three other wet people,
dripping and grouchy.
My full backpack clunks against the wall.

Do they suspect?
Can everybody in the elevator
feel my whole body loving this boy?

56

Myrtle & Annie have been bowling lately
starting with the Jesus Club and then other times.
They didn't even tell me.

But they were thinking about me.
"In that science class they teach you
we came from monkeys, right?" says Annie.
We're getting out of the showers after gym.
"Well, not exactly monkeys," I say. We get our towels.
"There's adaptation,
there's genetics,
there are fossils. . . ." We're shaking our hair out.
I didn't even notice
how Annie's voice was like a trap getting set.
I get started:
"You've seen a diagram of a whale flipper and a human hand?
How they're so alike?"
Myrtle shakes out her jeans, Annie stands still in her towel.
"And how the front of an elephant
is like the front of a butterfly?

And how we look in embryo? We look like a salamander,
we even have gill slits." I still didn't catch on.

"Evolution goes against God,"
Myrtle says in an announcing voice.
I think of her poor father, staring at the TV
with his hood over his head.
"I don't think so," I say. "What if it's all a great big plan
in the mind of God, you know? All the cells of everything,
in God's imagination?"
Annie checks with Myrtle in an instant signal
an onlooker would never catch,
only I knew from our years together.
Then she unloads:
"You're too big for your britches, LaVaughn."
It hit a part of me I had not thought to protect.
"You have your fancy classes now,
that bigtime Biology book."
I start to move my mouth—

"You got your over-smart friends,
your tutorial. You're getting *groomed*.
We seen you all in your hats,
you strut."
My brain races with everything but words,
my throat lumps up.

Myrtle tells me, "You're too good for Jesus. That's the worst."
This was too awful and too fast.
The shortage of air, my throat wouldn't open.
What does it mean? I kept asking myself,

faster than I could think.
I didn't catch on what I was getting accused for.
"Wait a minute—" I said. But they were gone.
I slumped to classes
and did work
but my head was bulging with hurt.
I went to the hospital and the white heaps of sheets
and I flapped them and folded them,
flapping and folding for hours,
my mind dizzy with horribleness.
But the flapping and folding
must have helped.

I go home telling myself I'll be OK.
It's not the first time we ever disagreed, Myrtle & Annie and me.
But we used to be so close we got our periods within hours.
Now theirs are still together, mine is a week apart.

57

Next morning it's hard to be reasonable,
I want to escape myself.
Patrick misspelled "photosynthesis" and "prothallium"
after I told him twice before, he's such a good thinker
he shouldn't do that, I said so.

He's wearing the green shirt today,
which is getting very thready at the sleeves.
He says, in his slow voice, "LaVaughn,
you think you're better than me."

I shake my head No
but my stomach goes like a rock.
He says, "Every day I help you,
I clean the slides, I check the spores,
you look at me like I'm a wall." His eyes don't blink.
"You told me I was ridiculous.
I asked you to the dance,
you wouldn't look me in the face."
I'm sinking on my lab stool.

"I gave you a Valentine
and you laughed. That was mean, LaVaughn."

"It was a funny Valentine, Patrick—
I—" And that word hangs right there.
He is right.

"I worked so hard to get here," he tells me,
each word takes its time,
"you couldn't count high enough,
all the foster families I lived in.
You couldn't dream the things I saw in my life.
And you treat me like I don't matter.
You are—what's the word?" He won't stop looking at me.

Can't he see me being sorry?
Can't he see I'm already so sorry
he doesn't have to say the rest of it?
I shake my head, guilty, my brain hurting.
"Disdainful. You're disdainful, LaVaughn.
That's what you do to me.
I hope you get something real bad, LaVaughn,
I really do." His eyes don't let go.

It felt sickening.
Even to say "I'm sorry" would be an insult.
Just yesterday I told myself I'd be OK.

I think of myself, Verna LaVaughn,
and she's dissolving,
someone I have never met.

Patrick turns his back,
reads in his Biology book
and makes gametophyte notes.

That would be why Jody stays away.
He keeps away from the meanness of me.
That was what Patrick meant: "Then it isn't your boyfriend."
I get to Grammar early, too ashamed to visit
along the hallway with anybody.
I hunch in my place, staring at the floor.
Ronell comes in, dumps her backpack down
and grins at me.

She does that one thing. She grins.

I open my mouth. I tell Ronell.
It comes out slowly at first, and then speeds up
till it's streaming. "And not only Myrtle & Annie,
we trusted each other for our whole lives,
but now Patrick too, he let me have it
so hard I thought my stomach would break
there on my lab stool. I am such a terrible person,
I didn't even think. Not even once.
I didn't even think how terrible. I didn't
imagine."

I don't mention Jody, he is sacred,
even though his life is at the middle of it all.

Pouring it out to Ronell
wilts me across the desk, I droop.

I was not even sure Ronell was the right person.
She had to be, there was nobody else.
"You want my honest opinion?" she says.
I've already heard too many, but she goes ahead:
"LaVaughn, I like you for being uppity. That's partly
why we're here. Right?"
"Huh?" I ask her.

"Here in this room we're obligated to be uppity.
That's our purpose here. We're supposed to change.
Those friends of yours can't appreciate you.
They don't know how."

I stay silent. The others come in for class.
Ronell finishes up with a surprise,
leaning way over in my face, confiding:
"I walked in here last fall saying 'ain't.'
By October I was telling my boyfriend
'Don't be so inert,' he broke up with me.
It's a price I pay."

"You didn't say anything about that," I whisper.
"No, I did not," she whispers back. "I had to weigh
my mixed feelings by myself. I had to get
some equilibrium about it. I had to do that."
Dr. Rose begins class
and I look over at Ronell,
and I think she is maybe half right.

58

I go home and there's Lester, as usual,
I can smell he has brought flowers, as usual. And
the kitchen stool. I try it out.
He's fixed it with brackets.

I hear my mom in her soft-cloth voice in the living room.
"Oh, Lester, that's too bad,
that's just too bad.
That shouldn't happen to such a nice person. . . ."
And Lester says back to her, "You think I'm nice?"
His voice glides.
"If I didn't, you wouldn't have a place at my supper table,"
says my mom, gentling him right back.

"How's school, LaVaughn?" he asks me in his visiting voice.
"Come on sit and talk to your mother and I."
He should say, "talk to your mother and me."
I say school is OK.
My life is so swollen with things,
I wouldn't know where to begin.

I take my books to my room
and I blow Jody in the photograph a kiss
and I ask him
in a voice of pitying myself
if he thinks I'm too uppity
and I get on my bed to face my homework,
even though I'm too upset to do any of it.
I try concentrating.
As usual, my door is shut all but a breath.

Soon there's a little burst, beginning with my mom.
"Harassing you? Lester, is that what I heard you say?
You are being harassed by the electric company
that wants their bill paid?"
She is going toward the top of her lungs.

Oh, boy, Lester.
Lester hasn't heard my mom
when somebody's jimmying with the facts.

I stay on my bed but I lean way over toward the door.
I don't want to miss this one. I move my math book off my lap
as my mom rises to her next level.
"They told you how many times to pay the bill?"
Lester says something I don't hear clearly.

She goes down a pitch:
"And there's the phone bill, too?
You said you paid that one, Lester. You told me you paid it.
You been calling me from a phone booth?"

And Lester makes his reply, again it is one I can't quite hear.
Lester is friendly and quiet.
And then my mom is not. She goes up several notches:
"You told me an untruth, Lester. Is that what you did?"
Uh-oh, Lester.

Now their voices go quite low
like people calmly working out a discussion.
I heave my math book back onto my lap.
But then the big one occurs,
and I can't help how my head pops.

It was so sudden I thought it was the TV,
not my mom at all.
"You have three minutes to collect your hat and coat
and the flowers you brought and walk out that door,
leave the key to it behind you on that table."
"What?" he said, like a movie also.
"I believe there is nothing wrong with your hearing, Lester.
Now, go."
There is a small sound of sofa cushions rising free of weight,
of shoes walking on the floor, a very slight jingle of keys.
And a tap of metal on wood.
The door opens.
The door closes.

Lester made it before his three minutes were up.
I continued sitting on my bed
quivering with the impact of such an uppity woman.

59

The last straw? I wanted so much
to change the subject of my own life,
I wanted her to hurt too, to keep me company.
I kept asking her, and asking.
She was rearranging the furniture,
dusting the shelf in the living room,
putting the ceramic wedding pot back in its place,
washed, dried, and empty.

It turns out Lester did the unthinkable,
not knowing it was.

Lester appreciated my mom for sure.
He appreciated her
the whole time he was bellying up to the table,
shoveling down her excellent chicken,
her tender fish, her yams, her macaroni,
her pizza from scratch,
her orange chiffon cake

with strawberries and real whipped cream,
her pecan crumb pie. Her yum-yum-yum food he appreciated
till my mom could hardly see straight.

What Lester didn't know was
he could have all the food he wanted,
all the warm, cozy, nice, clean house,
all the late-night phone calls about how valued
my mom was to him,
he might even get her to uproot me and move us out there
to the tree and the mud and the roof that needs replacing.

But he shouldn't go near mentioning
A LITTLE LOAN, A SMALL BORROWING
FROM LAVAUGHN'S COLLEGE SAVINGS ACCOUNT.

What were you THINKING, Lester?
Did you make the mistake of imagining you could
SIDETRACK MY MOM?

Lester,
that low form of life
who moved on with his friendly voice
and his high standards
to a different job
in a different office
where he'll find some big-hearted woman
to cook his supper,
praise him for bringing flowers,
believe him when he says

he'll bring her aunt a new hearing-aid battery,
a whole box of them that never shows up.
She'll think about moving to a house with him.
This man with his soft hands
and soft brain.
I listened while drawers and doors
opened and closed, while Mom got my dad out again
and put him back, his photographs everywhere.

But what she did then:
She ironed everything we have that's made of cloth.
She ironed my jeans. My underwear. Dishtowels.
She washed and ironed curtains,
nightgowns, sweatshirts, her bathrobe, my bathrobe.
She ironed pot holders and washcloths.
She didn't stop.

Late at night,
my brain cooked from homework
and from trying to understand my life
and wondering how I could have been
so awful without knowing it
I asked her,
"Mom, what are you doing?"
"I am ironing," she said.

60

(I felt like a parentheses.
Everything going on in the world
outside me:
Jody and his ambition and his mystery,
Myrtle & Annie, Patrick, Ronell,
my mom ironing to get hold of her self-respect,
everybody identifying things, deciding things,
getting mad at things and knowing why,
making up their minds.
And me the only one not.
I wanted to stay in my room
with my ceiling of green branches,
my little birds in their nest,
lie on my familiar bed, next to my blue bookcase,
beside my desk, near my shriveling orange from Jody,
my happy photograph of us on the wall.
I wanted to keep it all still,
and rest.
Let the whole world roll on by
outside my door.)

61

But how one day can change your life.
One minute. A tenth of a second of one minute.
If you'd done something else but what you actually did.

If Dr. Rose had not been sick in bed that day.
If I'd joined Cross Your Legs for Jesus
and gone to the club meeting.

If we had been out of chocolate chips.
If we hadn't had any orange rinds in the freezer compartment
to grate into the cookie dough.

But I baked.

It started when Jody's mom came up from their place
way before daylight,
she had his homework in her hand,
he couldn't be late with it and lose points.
He needs all the points he can get
for the swimming scholarship.
She wanted me to take his homework

to two separate teachers
and I said I would.
Jody's real sick, she said, fever and everything,
he can't go to school today.
It's just a bad cold, but still.

Jody's invisible handprints were on his math,
I stroked the pages with my fingers
in the groggy dark of the morning.

I put the homework in my pack along with all my stuff,
and I took it to his teachers
who thanked me and I explained Jody was sick.

In Biology Patrick and I were like two pencils in a box,
parallel but not alive to each other,
my guilty feelings stifling my common sense.
In gym Myrtle & Annie were so sideways to me,
their private looks detoured around me.
I felt lonely in the room with their Jesus jewelry,
I held my shampoo out to Myrtle like old times
but she shook her head no, she had brought her own.

Sirens ringing over the teachers' voices,
I go through the day
in a cell of isolation, my own private pod.
I went to the hospital early and got off early,
thinking about Jody, how we'd go to college
together and graduate in those black caps and gowns
and get jobs and he'd see how perfect I am for him.

I was home earlier than I would be.
It seemed the most natural thing: Bake Jody
some get-well cookies.

I have asked over and over again:
When I could have done so many different things:
an extra Biology lab, an extra hospital shift,
to get me closer to college. Anything.
If I had done what I should have done:
find Patrick in the Biology lab after school,
apologize to him, as I could not do in class
with his face turned away from me
and other people all around.

Instead I softened the butter,
creamed it with white and brown sugar,
beat in the vanilla and egg,
sifted the flour and soda and salt into the bowl,
grated the frozen orange peel into it
(frozen is easier to grate)
along with adding the chocolate chips
and walnuts, which I like to break up with my hands.
Maybe raisins, too? I asked myself.
It seemed to be an interesting question.

While the cookies were in the oven,
I made a card with red, blue, and green markers
on notebook paper:
a cartoon of him lying in bed
with a thermometer sticking out of his mouth.

It wasn't very original.
I felt embarrassed about that
thinking I should have more imagination.

When the cookies had cooled I put them on a plate,
placing each cookie in alignment with the others
in a concentric pattern.

I laid the card on top of the cookies.
I stretched plastic wrap over the whole thing
and attached it underneath.

I'd sneak in softly, using my key,
not to disturb the sick patient,
I'd put the cookies right beside the fish tank in the living room,
right where I put the dance photograph.
Jody would be so HAPPY.
He'd run his fingers over the silly drawing on the card
and he'd smile.
Among such confusing events in my life
this would be one good thing.
I felt generous and clear.
As Dr. Rose says, lucid.

I carry the plate of cookies and my keys,
I take the elevator down three floors,
a crumpled woman in the elevator
looks at the cookies and she says,
"You're a good girl, LaVaughn."
I pull the plastic up on one side and give her two cookies.
She says it again. "You're a good girl, LaVaughn."

I get out and I go down Jody's hall
wishing somebody would replace the burnt-out light.

I put the key in their bottom lock and turn it. Almost no sound.
Then I put it in the top lock. Almost no sound.
My heart was beating too hard, because of the sneaking.
I got their door open almost in silence,
balancing the plate of cookies on the flat of my left hand.

I'll remember till my dying day
that I wondered if the cookies might slip,
ruining the design.

I had a slow but sure momentum,
walking slightly into the dim room, balancing the plate,
holding the door not to slam with my other hand.

The first thing I saw was the lamplight on the fishtank,
and two people, just their heads
partly hidden behind the tank.
Like they were whispering to each other.
I got my eyes to focus and
there was something in my spine pulling me back
but something in my eyes pushing me forward
and I recognized Jody but not the other one,
I only noticed it was a boy.
I stood ice-still and I saw their mouths go together and stay
and I froze.
The plate of cookies
went straight onto the rug
and my lifetime jumped upside down.

I could not be LaVaughn anymore.
This could not be my life.
I backed out the door
and I halfway got it closed
but then I took off
running.

I don't remember the elevator ride,
maybe I took the stairs,
I don't remember coming in our door.
Walking. Anywhere.

I do remember remembering
sometime late in the darkness under my pillow on my bed
that I had to clean up the baking mess.
My mom would come home and ask where the cookies were.

I remember making myself get up.
I remember seeing a mixing bowl and a cookie sheet
in soapsuds in front of me.
I remember a blue sponge cleaning the counter.
It must have been in my hand.

Yes, that blue sponge must have been in my hand.

Part Four

62

I burst wide awake and the clock says 3:14 A.M.
My mind says maybe it didn't happen.
Maybe if I go back down there
Jody will be doing his homework
munching on cookies
snuffling with his cold.

I fought off
the sight of Jody and that boy,
pretending he is still the same Jody
who showed me how to shift my weight on a skateboard,
who danced with me.
But there were those two heads in the lamplight.
My throat was so lumped up
I knew I couldn't unknow what I knew.

I went to my closet
with scissors in my hand
and I cut my blue crushed velvet dress
up the middle, laid it open like a wound.
I never did such a thing as that before in my life.

I stared at the slashes.
I did not feel any better for it.

That was what Patrick meant:
"Then it's not your boyfriend."
By 5:26 A.M. those faces and the fish tank
filled my dark bedroom like a movie
I couldn't help seeing.

63

School was out of the question. My mind
was a wreckage, with parts all thrown about
and no clear view of front, back or sideways.

My mom wakes me as usual
and the only safe place is under the covers.
I do what I never did before: I tell her I can't go to school.
"You what?" she says, dangerous and quiet. I say it again.
"You sick?" she wants to know.
"No," I tell her, poking my head to the edge.
"I'm not sick, my mind is in an uproar
and I need to get it calmed down,
it is in shock." Each time I talked the lump crowded in.
I put my head back down in the dark.

She stands in the doorway
and she says, "That's too bad, what a disappointment.
Tell me, LaVaughn, you like the color blue?"

"Why?" I say. Those two boys behind the fishtank.
"Just do you like blue? In a car? Would a blue car be nice?"

What does she mean, I ask,
my head still in the dark under the blankets.
"Well, LaVaughn, you can't go to high school for one day,
you *sure* can't go to college for four years. That's real sad,
and I'm thinking how to spend your college account
you won't be needing.
I'm real tired of riding the bus.
A blue car would be nice."

I pull my head out into the cold air.
If I had other girls' mothers I could stay home.
With those two heads behind the fishtank
right in the middle of my brain
I get out of bed.

I saw that I was in my pajamas.
I didn't remember putting them on.
I would never face Jody again in my life.

I already knew how to avoid his schedule
going through side doors and back ways.
But everything was inside out now.
Two boys kissing. Would I dream such a thing?
No. The kitchen was washed up just the way I left it.

I stripped the covers off my notebooks
and put the pages in folders instead.
I threw the covers in the Dumpster.

I thought about the walking suicide kids,
how they look like everybody else.

They eat breakfast, go to school,
go in the bathroom and overdose or shoot themselves.
They are in the news. I always wondered,
what could they be thinking?
I never understood. Now I do.

64

I wanted to be numb
dumb
a rock.
I would rather be a pebble
than be LaVaughn.

How can life just keep going on?
Why doesn't everything come to a stop?

Not an hour goes by but it's Jody's eyes, voice, feet,
Jody's hand in his back pocket the way he stands.
And those faces behind the fishtank,
the lump in my throat the size of a house.

During math he swims between my legs,
looking over my shoulder
the way he did.

Classes feel like imitations.
Myrtle & Annie have three other girls in gym
to laugh with,

they have matching "Know Your Limits" wristbands,
I notice without taking it in.
Jody is walking around somewhere in this same building I am.
Patrick looks at my notebook pages loose in folders,
noticing where I tore the "Jody Jody Jody" covers off,
he looks away. He keeps his back turned.
I look at our fern spores but I am not curious about them.

In Grammar Build-Up I don't meet eyes with Dr. Rose.
She says "enriching your lives"
and she says "abundance of ideas."
She says, "Defining moments present themselves to us,
often disguised,
when we must make momentous decisions
that shape our lives."
I want to scream. I don't say a word. The Brain Cells
have never seen me like this. I'm holding on
with my fingernails. Any moment I'll lose that meager grip
and my skin will fall away.

Their faces catch on
and they cover for me.
Doug says low, so only the four of us hear,
"It'll pass, LaVaughn.
It's bad but it'll pass." I look at my hands
clenched in my lap,
I am like the crazy, mumbling people on the street.
Doug makes me put both hands up with theirs
in our team clutch. I don't care.
I didn't even thank him with my face.

65

What would you do?
I took sheets and pillowcases to the oncology floor.
I held Lee Anne's hand.

I think I moved like a ghost.
My life was not visible
to the naked eye.
But I heard my feet
in the corridors.

I was still going on
when I thought just hours ago I couldn't.
I was doing what I couldn't do.

66

I only wanted to go to my room,
stay there till kingdom come.

But our old neighbor we've had since I can't remember when
caught me with my key in my hand
just at the door.
She shuffled out from her door
bringing with her a pink rose in a vase
with a gauzy purple ribbon sticking out.
She says a florist delivered it.
It has my name on a little envelope pinned to the ribbon.
That is Jody's writing.
My heart goes like a barrel turning over.

She asks if it's my birthday,
she says Happy Birthday to me,
I tell her no, I stare at that rose,
and I think how I want to die.
I tell our old neighbor thank you
and she smiles at my happy juvenile life,
her wrinkled eyes all lit up for my nice youth.

I heave my backpack up from where it has slid down,
I take the plastic vase from her
and I unlock the door
to our apartment, exactly the same as Jody's.
Over there where he has the fishtank
we have the couch and a crooked little table
all marked up from being old.

This is the home I brought Jeremy to
when Jilly had to go to the hospital
and I wondered how their lives would turn out.
Now it is my life that won't turn out.
I want to close my eyes and have it be gone.

In my room I put the vase with the rose in it on my desk.
I lie down on my bed.
I stare at the birds' nest on my ceiling and I sing
the words, "Willow, weep for me," that old song.
I tried to blank my mind
but it wouldn't. The mind is such a busy thing,
opinionating and asking,
my exercising head wouldn't let go.

I could only see Jody and that boy, their heads
kissing in the half-light.
I would never open that envelope.

> "Ha ha LaVaughn, it was all a joke."
> "It was a plan to have you walk in my door and be
>   jealous."

>*"We rigged it so you would come in, none of it was real."*
>*"I really love you, LaVaughn."*
>*"Are you mad at me, LaVaughn?"*

My brain wouldn't let go.

67

I left the envelope pinned to the ribbon.
Days went by, the rose wrinkled and drooped down.

Annie's face came into my mind
not liking Jody for so long
and joining that club.
I would tell her, I was that mad.
No. No, I wouldn't.
No, I would never tell Annie. Nor Myrtle either.
I would not be such a mean human being to do that.

That drying rose and that wrinkled orange
stood on my desk like sneers.
The photograph from the dance I put with Jody's key
in the bottom of a shoebox
in the bottom of my closet
underneath my cut dance dress hanging in shreds.
Down there it would be gone out of my life.
But not really.

I went sneaking around back doorways, hiding
but I still wanted to know that photograph was there.

68

What happens next:
My mind was such a swamp of horrible distress
I ruined the Biology quiz,
I didn't get questions 25, 26, and 29,
and when I looked at my grade on my paper
it felt like the end coming to get me.

The end of what?
The end of trusting my own mind,
or the end of ever expecting a boy to love me,
the end of expecting to go to college,
the end of any good feeling ever.

How did I botch everything so badly
all by myself?
How did I let my own life get away from me?

69

On my way up to The Children's Hospital
I stopped to watch a shiny beetle
creeping along the sidewalk, leg by leg.
It came to a big pebble in its way, stopped,
waited for something, some nerve impulse maybe,
adjusted its position and went around to the right.

I said the Greek name of its order: *Coleoptera*.
These are more highly evolved than cockroaches.
The beetle kept pacing along,
it came to one of those cracked-out places
that sidewalks have,
scraped and broken
like a small excavation. The beetle crept down into it,
pushing along, millimeter by millimeter,
and when it came to where it had to climb up again,
it paused for another moment,
and then it climbed.

I said to myself, LaVaughn, imagine if you were this beetle,
with all the feet and bikes and skateboards

and in a few minutes it will try to cross the street
and along will come the Number 9 bus
and splat.
And the whole tragedy came over me.
The whole thing. How life is so thin and fragile,
how you never know. One instant you're here
and then you're gone.

Jody.
Myrtle & Annie.
Patrick and his hard life.
My dad gone forever.
Jilly and Jeremy never even had their dads look at them.
The children in the hospital,
Lee Anne waiting maybe forever,
others with bald heads from chemo,
their legs skinny and weak,
playing with games in the brightly colored playroom
and soon dying.
Everything is tragic.
Why didn't anybody ever tell me that before?

I spent all those months with Jilly and Jeremy
and didn't even figure it out.
Couldn't I have looked in my mom's face
and seen it?
Couldn't I have understood
without having to find out now?

70

The Guidance Man calls me in,
the one who moved me around before
and said I should come to him with my questions.
He is in his office with his necktie on and his education look.
He wants me to "account for my lack of consistency."
He says, "LaVaughn, we have gone out on a limb for you,
we believe in your future," and he reminds me
how he lifted me out of a plain science class into a harder one.

I have no way to tell him life is a whole tragedy
which I just found out.
I sit there.

"LaVaughn, do you want to go to college?" he says.
If life is only a tragedy, why would I want to go to college?
But it is that word again, the one I made so important
all these years:
I never didn't want to go to college,
how could I start now?

I tell him Yes, I've wanted to go to college since fifth grade.
"Then we want to help you get there. We can't have
any more of these unstable grades. Is that clear, LaVaughn?"
I could tell him how unstable everything is,
the whole tragic world,
but suddenly it is not such a tragedy.
College.
"Yes, it's clear," I tell him and I mean it so much.
"I do want to go to college. Maybe be a nurse?"
In that man's office it just came out.
I didn't even know I thought it.
This same person who would die because of Jody
now wants to go to college and be a nurse.
Life is too strange, my brain must be insane.

"A nurse?" He is interested.
I tell him I work up at The Children's Hospital
and how it is there. I tell him about Lee Anne,
I tell him I have seen crack babies.
He leans forward in his chair.
"LaVaughn, would you like
to have a Career Tour of the Nursing School?"
I have to say something.
Did he mean I could be a nurse?
"Well, maybe not a real nurse.
Maybe a nurse's aide?
Maybe a helper with sick little kids?"
"Oh, yes, a real nurse," he says.
"Why not?" he says. He is not kidding.
"Why not?" he says again, asking himself.

It all came out too fast,
I hadn't thought it through. "Oh, I don't know."
I had just done very bad school work
and now here I was talking about being a nurse.

"LaVaughn, I will personally check your Biology grades
every single week. Personally.
You want to be a nurse,
we'll do everything we can to get you there.
You do your part.
I will personally check your grades.
Go now." He stands up and reaches out his hand to shake.
"Deal?" he says.
I put my hand out and shake his.
I have not shaken many different hands before.
"Deal," I say.

He says, "LaVaughn. Stop right there. Put out your hand.
Let's do that handshake again." I put out my hand.
"Harder," he says. What does he mean?
"Grip my hand harder."
I do it.

"No, harder. There, that's it. Now keep your eyes on my face."
I look at him.
"No, you don't just glance and then look away.
Keep your eyes looking at me.
Grip hard.
Shake.
Keep looking at me."
This is so strange.

He lets my hand go and he smiles so big.
"You're going to be a nurse, you need a firm handshake,
not a weak little flap,
you need to look them in the eye when you shake their hand."
I nod my head.
"You see what I mean?"

I say yes and I go.
So is life one whole tragedy or not?

71

Then it was the Biology teacher
telling me to stay after class.
I had tried to keep away from her,
and Patrick kept his back turned all the time,
we checked our fern spores separately,
we didn't even brush sleeves with each other.
I had already looked up my wrong quiz answers,
some were way off and some were only a little off.
"Backsliding is dangerous, LaVaughn,
backsliding is like quicksand. You know?"

And in that look in her face
the tragedy got bigger and worse.
But then:
"And LaVaughn, we're having a Career Tour
of the Nursing School in two weeks.
Will you sign up?"

Not only the Guidance Man.
This woman, too?
My dirty neighborhood,

this dangerous school, my tragic life,
my bad, bad grade.

"Say you want to go, LaVaughn." I don't get it, but
it might be my very last chance.
"Whom do I sign up with?" I say.
She imitates me. "*Whom* do you sign up with?"
"I said it wrong?" I say.
"No! No! Not at all! It's wonderful! Whom!
Then you want to go?" Now she's smiling at me.
I nod my head.
"Good for you," she says.

My nerve was up. I asked her.
"How come you ask me such a thing?
About the Nursing School tour?
When I got such a bad grade on the quiz?"

Her eyes got fierce. "Because.
LaVaughn, don't you have any idea?
Don't you get it?
We have some serious students,
some brave, determined kids
in this neighborhood—"
and she takes hold of my arm there on her desk.
And her voice goes husky, nearly down to a whisper:
"We can't lose you. Not one of you.
We can not let you slip away."

72

Patrick. His name came out of the air
when I woke up the next morning.
Maybe I could do something about Patrick.
I could try to be a human being to him.

I wanted it all to go away,
I wanted not to do any of it.
Instead I marched into Biology
and I said in a low voice to his back, just above whispering,
"Listen, Patrick, I know you won't speak to me.
I'll speak to you." I knew the words,
they came swimming up
from way far below where they must have been waiting.
He continues reading his book on the lab counter. I go on.
"You were right. I was wrong.
I was terrible. I was mean. I was insulting. You're so smart,
you're smart enough to turn around at least."
Hunched over in the brown sweatshirt, he didn't move.
I made myself not stop.
"Patrick," I keep on keeping my voice low.
"I'm sorry."

There is a slight budge of his shoulders.
Hardly any.
Then his page turns. His feet move,
slowly he turns around on his lab stool.
He looks at me with his steady eyes. "Me too," he says.

I felt the air get warmer.
I had said I was sorry
and he had said "Me too." That is a lot.
We looked at each other
and his slow smile came up partly
and he said, "You want to do echinoderms?"
I nodded my head yes. I got on my stool
and got my book out
and we began echinoderms and I felt a little bit mature
and so relieved
I was shaking.

We did the part about how these starfish and sea urchins
probably evolved from a bilateral ancestor, and
now that I knew him better
I asked about the cross around his neck.
"The nuns gave it to me.
I just never took it off," he says.
"It seemed like if they cared enough
to feed me all those years
I could wear the cross they gave me."

"All those years?" I say.
"Yeah. Every time a foster home turned bad
the nuns took me back.

They liked me 'cause I wasn't sassy
and I was good in math."
Patrick has big sincere eyes:
I imagine him a little kid,
going back to the nuns with his bag of clothes.
"They safety pinned my mittens to my coatsleeves," he says
with his smile of trusting.

"What does the cross mean?" I ask him.
"Crucifix. I don't know exactly. Jesus hanging in agony,
nailed to boards. But it's a reminder."
"Of what?"
"Well. Of— Well, evil.
That evil's always gonna be around,
and you deal with it."
"What about evolution?" I ask him.
"What about it?" he says.
"Does the Bible say it isn't true?"
Patrick laughs. "Of course not. Who told you that?"

I suddenly want to protect Myrtle & Annie
from being laughed at. "Never mind who.
But doesn't evolution go against the Bible?"
Patrick rolls his eyes. "Not at all.
Only if you take everything word for word for word.
The Bible is really funny about time.
You know, guys living for centuries—
Noah lived to be 930 years old—
women having babies in their 90s,
the universe being created in 6 days.
The Bible isn't a calendar. It's a book of stories

and lessons. And I bet the nuns told me every one of them.
Over and over again."

"Hmmm," I said.
Then I asked, "Do you go to church?"
Patrick says, "Well, yeah, part of the time.
Sometimes not. Why?"
"I just wondered. Let's do the starfish."

In Grammar Build-Up I continued asking.
"Ronell, do you go to church?"
"Sometimes, yeah. Why?"
"I'm wondering about God."
"Then don't ask me.
I don't know anything about God," she says.

"Well, what do you *think* about God?" I push.
"Oh, I don't know. Maybe God is the beginning.
The start of protons. The first breath of anything. Maybe."
"But you don't know for sure?"
"Not really," she says. "How could anybody know really?"
"Then why do you go to church?"
"Oh, my mom makes me go.
I keep hoping it'll make sense
and I'll catch on. And I like the music.
Listen, LaVaughn, what was wrong with you?
The other day. When you were so out of yourself?
What was that?"

I tell her I can't tell her.
I could not say what I saw in Jody's house

to Ronell, if I let it out of my mouth
it will have to be true.
"You sure?" she says.
"Ronell, I am too sure for words."
"Well, you change your mind,
you can tell me. You hear?"

It is easier to ask about God
than to think about Jody.
Doug and Doc walk in
and I ask them.
Doug says he doesn't believe in God
and I ask why and he says there's too much evil
in the world, no God would let such evil happen.
Doc is different, he is undecided.
"I wouldn't say there *isn't* a God,
but I wouldn't say there is, either.
No convincing evidence on either side."
"Well, what about evolution, then?" I say.
Ronell says what Patrick said. "Evolution and the Bible
don't cancel each other out."
"Well, I'm just asking," I say.
"Here's an example," says Doug.
"Religions have all got some big truth all their own,
and they don't know who to blame
for the evil they see
so they blame each other—"
Doc interrupts. "And every time anybody fights a war,
they say God's on their side.
Holy wars. That's religion for you."

Dr. Rose appears at our chairs by radar:
"Brain Cells one and all, I admire your discourse,
but one of you has misplaced a 'whom,'" she says,
and she moves to another group.

I was asking everybody else,
so why not my mom, too?
"Oh, sure, we went to church,
me and your daddy. So did you.
You went to Sunday School."
"And then?" I ask.
"Oh, then church got too lonely.
And the music always made me cry.
So I stopped."

She stays silent for a few minutes.
"I still have your Sunday School dress," she says.
"In a box."

This is news to me. With everything in my life
so strange and untrustable
I did not expect a little dress out of my past.
Before I know it
she has washed and ironed it
and it hangs on the shower rod:
yellow, ruffled, and size 4.
I put my face in it, trying to remember
who I was back then, how I talked,
anything. All I get is a feeling of textures.
Being fed and combed and tucked in bed.

And how my mom held my hand every single time
we went out our door. I want to be quiet,
holding the little dress, trying to remember.

My mom puts in her big voice:
"You think I'd get through one day of raising you
if I wouldn't of had help from God?
Think about it, LaVaughn."

I spend hours in my room
going over it all, staring at the leathery rose on my desk,
going over it all again.
There was too much of it.
Besides everything else,
all those people in Hell
if Myrtle & Annie's church is right:
All those people I love.
I kept trying to think it through.

73

Just after lunch
grabbing books from my locker
I quick turned my head
and Jody was in my face
right there
walking by—
his silky, irresistible eyes looked straight at me
of all the places he could have looked
or I could have.
In another world I would have
held him close with my arms
and kissed his mouth.
We would have danced together till the end of time.

In this world I looked away from him
at the backs of strangers
and he walked on,
a normal-looking person in a T-shirt
who had sent a rose to a girl
who never opened the card.

It took me all of math class to stop trembling.

74

It was a sudden impulse. The church I pass
on my way home from the hospital
is always the same, with often a homeless person
reading a magazine on the stone steps.
I got off the bus there instead of coming right home.
It was near dark, and I naturally wondered
where that homeless one would sleep.
I walked up the steps and went in through the heavy door.

In there it was quiet, no city sounds came through
and somebody was running a dust mop
under the benches. He comes right over to me,
carrying the mop with him.
A medium man in a sweater and glasses,
he tells me he's the minister.
I don't know what to ask,
and from somewhere sideways in my mind
out came Myrtle & Annie's play.
I blurt, "If a girl had an abortion,
could she come to this church?"

It was not my urgent question
but it would stall while my courage came to me.

He took off his glasses
and said, "Of course. We're here to help you."
"It's not me, I just was wondering."
"Everyone is welcome here," he said in a believable voice.
"Would you like to know about our youth services?
Right over here, our schedules, our bulletins,
our calendars, our youth ministry,"
he puts his glasses back on, holds the mop in one hand,
and we go over to the side of the church where there's a table
with neat piles of papers in different colors.
He begins to hand me several.

"And another thing," I go on ahead,
hoping this place is as private as it feels.
"Would you let—do you have any—"
I hear my voice going softer—
"Can any— could any gay people come here? Or not?
Or do gay people go to Hell?
You wouldn't—there's no—is there a—
or—oh, never mind. Never mind. Here, I'll take these,
thanks—" I start to leave.

But this minister slows me down. "Of course.
We welcome everyone.
We're mere human beings.
God doesn't turn anyone away,
and neither do we."

He looks at me, a gay girl who wants an abortion.
"We weren't put on Earth to exclude each other," he says.
He smiles at me in such a friendly way,
I would almost go to this church. I take a chance:
"But how do you know for sure? About God or anything?"
He leans on the dust mop handle. "We can only hope.
We can only be as sure as our faith."

"Thanks," I say, rolling up the colored papers,
"I have to go home now."
"Thank you for coming in," he says. "Go in peace."
I head for the door.
"Young woman?" he says. I turn around.
"If there is a Hell,
it's when we stop caring about each other.
We wouldn't wish that on anyone."
He waves his hand, lifts the dust mop
and heads back where he was.

"Go in peace."
I don't remember anybody
ever saying that to me before.

75

They got my name on the list for the Nursing School Tour
and my mom lights up with excitement about it.
"I never thought. My own daughter.
I never thought. That's an honor, Verna LaVaughn,
good for you." This is a good thing
coming out of all the bad things
and for a few minutes I throw all the freakish
horribleness aside and congratulate myself.

I go to my room
filled with those Jody objects
and look in the closet
making sure I really did that with the scissors.
There it is, its insides all exposed,
a ruined dress, humiliated
with Jody's invisible handprints on its back.

I spread my homework on my desk
and my mom's voice comes through my door,
all simple with innocence:

"I was sure we had chocolate chips.
LaVaughn, you know what happened to the chocolate chips?

"LaVaughn, you answer me.
Where's your manners? I *asked*
about the chocolate chips, where they went." Her tone rises.
"LaVaughn, did you eat a whole bag of chocolate chips?
There's carrots here, and oranges, you could eat grapes.
LaVaughn!"

All the time I knew this would happen,
I could have bought a bag of chocolate chips,
why didn't I?
From that day the cookie plate dropped down on the floor
I could not face a chocolate chip.
I go to the kitchen. I sit on the stool.
"I used the chocolate chips."
I wanted to avoid this forever and yet
I have let her find out.

"Why didn't you say so?" She is impatient.
I don't know how to tell her this is beyond impatience,
this is worse
than chocolate chips.

"Why didn't you just say so?
I asked, you were in your room, you heard me."
It's my starting to cry that stops her going on
in this regular way
about something that is not regular.

230

"Something's up. LaVaughn.
Look at me, LaVaughn.
I can think of a hundred things might bother you.
You make it easy, you tell me which one it is.
Verna LaVaughn."

I look at her, she is blurry through my tears.
"You'd never guess this one," I say. "Not ever."
"LaVaughn, I heard most things in my life.
Tell me." She comes over to me, puts her arms around me,
"Tell your mama, honey."

I haven't said it out loud before,
in hope of making it not true.

I never said anything like it before.
"I baked cookies for Jody, he was sick,
I wanted him to love me like a girlfriend,
I took the cookies down there,
a boy was kissing him on the mouth,
he was kissing him back."
My crying got so big I hardly noticed
what my mom's body did,
but later I remembered plain as day,
her body expanded then contracted.
A big breath heaved her to her full strength of a mother
like a wall to lean on.

I hope if I cry hard enough it'll go away,
I hope there's a God and God will make it unhappen.

Nobody says anything for a long time.
I cry and I cry and she holds me.
"LaVaughn, I tell you. I don't know
how it feels
down there in your heart
where it hurts so bad.
I never had *that* kind.
But you just sit here
and you cry
and I won't go away."

And I did so. I did all the crying Jeremy and Jilly did
in that whole year I was with them.
I can even draw a diagram of the lachrymal gland.

I couldn't stop. And my mom didn't leave.
She reached behind her
to turn down the heat
under a pot on the stove, but she did not lose her touch on me.

Maybe it was hours she held me there, maybe only minutes.
And then she fed me supper in bed,
her good beef and mushrooms,
she pulled up a chair to my desk and we ate there in my room
with the weeping willow tree hanging over.

Mostly I was too emptied out to do anything but barely eat.
"You got your appetite, you'll live,"
my mom tries to make a joke.
It was not funny.
That dead pink rose in the florist vase

is pushed to the back of my desk.
My mom says, "You should open that card some day."

I look down at my supper.
Maybe I will, maybe I won't.
"I cut my dress," I said. It sounded
like childish pride in doing such a thing.
"My dress from the dance."
I tilt my head toward the closet.
She puts her supper plate on my desk,
gets up, walks over and looks
at the dress I bought with my college money,
makes a little tiny gasp,
comes back to her chair
picks up her plate again. She nods her head
and nobody says a word.

We go along eating, only the sound of forks.
I take a couple of bites and watch the juice
drift around the plate.
A siren goes by down on the street.
My mom lets the silence be. Then,
"LaVaughn, would you like a birthday party?"
I couldn't live through a party.
I tell her no.
"LaVaughn, you listen here.
We could make a Sweet Sixteen for you,
every girl should have one. It's a—"
My mom put her plate down, she came over to my bed,
she put her arms around me all over again,
she said down in my face, "Oh, honey,

this is so hard. So hard. I know that.
Maybe a party would make you feel better?
Streamers and cake?"

I just wanted to be there,
with my mom's arms around me,
letting her try to convince me
for a while.
It was a terrible time but
I was not as out of balance as before.

Would Myrtle & Annie even come
to my party? Then why have one? But maybe?

By the time we had dessert
of sour-cream-apple pudding I knew my answer.

76

But I was so suspicious of hope.
Sitting in the park
feeding cafeteria bread discards to the pigeons
I made my list
for my 16th birthday party
that I had thought about through the years of my life.
Now I wondered if anyone would come.

Would Myrtle & Annie? The Brain Cells? Patrick?
Jolly, Jilly, and Jeremy? And their Ricky?

It was an odd combination of people,
I had to admit.

I didn't know whether or not
my heart was completely broken in pieces
as I threw bits of bread to those many pigeons.
Rock doves, actually. *Columba livia.*
Phylum chordata, subphylum vertebrata, class Aves.
On the downstroke of their wings
the edge of each wing feather curls up

and they can fly away from terror,
their little tiny cerebrum forgetting what it was
that scared them so.

I don't know anything but this: That lump
the one in my throat
that knocks me around with its comings and goings
that lump was there when I went to sleep that night,
asking some kind of God
why this was all happening to me.
When I woke up the next day
all these bad events were still happening
but the lump was gone.

And so I came on the discovery
with no warning.
Religion must be for trusting.
And trusting, what is that for?
I figured it out: It helps you go on
when you can't go on.

77

On the Nursing School Tour
I pretended I was already there.
I even liked the uniforms, the fast quiet walking,
the bottles and gloves. The words: renal, neuro.

There were fifteen of us, from two different schools,
only a few I had ever seen, two from Biology
I knew by sight.
And one from Grammar.

The tour leader told about fibrillation and defibrillation
and the laser technician job.
We saw a cardiac monitor and how it works,
and they said we have to take chemistry
or we should already be in it. I am not.
I tried to hide behind a fat boy when they said that,
in case they would check.

They said Emergency takes a strong stomach
and nerves of steel, it is not for the squeamish,
they often have blood spurting there and diabetic coma

and many drug ODs.
And we went to Pediatrics,
the very same building where I work, I felt I knew
some of the advanced knowledge they were telling us.
But that's absurd. I'm only in laundry.
We walked the very same floors where I walk,
and they pointed out the familiar places:
the Pediatric Intensive Care Unit, they call it the PICU ,
the exam rooms, Radiology.
They said words I know already: spina bifida, otolaryngology,
epidural, ophthalmoscope, cardiomyopathy.
And everywhere we went
there were sickness and wellness side by side
and people trying to make one into the other.

How could I get to be one of them?
Could I even think of such a thing?

It got to be a rushing question in my ears
so I didn't even hear some of the guide's talk.
Just in my head over and over again:
Would it be so impossible?

On the bus home I thought
how there had to be nurses in Emergency
when my father died of a gunshot. Those nurses
saw him last of all. To them he was a patient that died.
One more heart that stopped.

Did they even know he had a little girl?

78

Of all the things I want
which do I want most?
College, as I have said all along?
Jody?
An explanation of how life is?
Myrtle & Annie to like me again?
To be a nurse for little kids?
Yes to all of them.
It's too much to ask. Even if there is a God.

Which could I not live without?
Look at my mom. She lives.
Without hardly anything. My dad was not perfect,
she admits. He was ornery and he left things lying around
and was stubborn
and they loved each other the whole time
and when I was born tears fell down his face.
And then she ended up with him dead from a gun
and she has just me,
a big kid who is both blessing and curse.
You look at your mother
and you have to ask: A life like that, could I live it?

79

Every single one of them says they'll come to my party.
Jolly will even bring Ricky.

Maybe it was the Nursing School Tour
that made me do what I had to do
with Myrtle & Annie. I couldn't not do it.
I tell them I don't think I'm too good for Jesus.
I tell them I didn't mean to strut.
I tell them I am so sorry I was rude.
Their eyes aren't sympathetic to my excuses.

"LaVaughn, you get all good chances
with your new classes, but you don't know,
it might be Satan getting you." Annie.
"If you'd come this afternoon
we could start getting you saved." Myrtle.

I don't want them praying for me to their opinionated God.
Instead I say, "Come to my party anyway?"
Myrtle & Annie say to each other,
right in front of me: "The limits?"

"The limits, well, it's LaVaughn. . . ."
"What about the limits?"
And I burst in. "Listen here.
We've been together since—what do you mean, limits?"

They stun me: "We're sposed to limit our contact
with non-Christians."

"Why?" My voice is not nice.

"It's too hard for God to get through
when there's clutter. Non-Christians are distracting."
Annie, my oldest friend, is embarrassed with me.

My heart rate goes up. I don't wait
for the right thing to say.
"Contact? *Con*tact?
I am not a *con*tact, I am your friend all these years.
We read comic books under the covers together.
I am not a contact. How can you say that?"
For the first time I actually notice their wristbands:
"Know Your Limits." That's what those words mean:
They mean to leave me out.

And then Myrtle goes soft first, and she says,
"LaVaughn, it's your party, I'll come."
She hasn't gentled up completely, but a little.
"Me too," says Annie, "it's your Sweet 16."
For a moment I see how mixed I am about them.
Sometimes it is so awful about friends.
Isn't it? I'm mad and clumsy about it
and so are they.

80

I don't know anything about anything.
I have been a chump and a fool.
Some days things add up,
other days I know I was put on the wrong planet.

But here is something. When my mom moved
all my dad's photographs back to their rightful places,
even finding one more
showing him with his Saturday basketball buddies,
when she put these pictures back where they belong
something was better.

She even said he came to her in a dream,
nice and smiling, telling her, "That was pretty dumb,
wasn't it?" That was all he said.
But she knew what he meant.

I wouldn't know how to believe in that.
And I can't believe like Myrtle & Annie
and I haven't found anything that feels exactly right
to believe in, but I believe

anyway. In something. That jellyfish I told about
and other astonishing things in science.
At night I put my things together in my backpack
and tell myself I can make it through another day.
Even in rainy, soppy, sloshy weather
in the freezing cold early hour of the morning
when I'm waiting at the bus stop
with old bent and frowning people,
I even feel my arms and legs being strong.

I believe in possibility.
In the possibility of
possibility.
Of the world making sense someday.

That lump in my throat
that keeps coming back to remind me of my messes:
It only stays for a little while.

I'm a true believer.
And that's a fact.

81

Summer Science Recruitment
came as an enormous surprise.
It happened because I got a good score
on the Science Aptitude Test. Which was a surprise too.

I can still keep my laundry job up at The Children's Hospital,
they'll even give me more hours for summer.
And I can go to Summer Science too,
a science class all day three days a week.
It teaches you how to understand Chemistry
and some Microbiology
so you won't be so far behind people at the good schools.
They teach it at an institute with six real labs,
way at the other end of town. They give you a bus pass.
You have to promise you won't drop out.
Patrick is going, too, and Doc,
and Ronell,
who took the test last year,
is going again for her second time.
Patrick scored 12th highest in the whole city.

The Biology teacher announced it because Patrick wouldn't.
He already knows he wants to be a brain researcher,
and with his smart brain he can be one.

In the interview
they ask a dozen questions from the government
which gave money for Summer Science,
and the other half came from a rich anonymous person.
Do I need grant money assistance
for notebook and pencils? I tell them no, I don't need that.
And for my lab fees? No again.
My mom would have a fit
at such a handout.

But she said this class
is a gift from heaven, and she signed the form
sitting in extra-straight posture.

The Guidance Man looked me hard in the face.
"LaVaughn, we're counting on you. Summer Science
may make the difference for you."
He says it's a good thing they found me.
"Another year and I believe it would have been too late."
He tests my handshake again. I pass.
He grins. "I'll be checking on you," he says.

With Summer Science coming
Sometimes a whole morning goes by
when I don't think about Jody.
This astounds me: How could he have gotten lost inside me?

At night, all alone, I hear myself repeating from Dr. Rose:
"I will rise to the occasion
which is life." I don't think I get it. But I say it.

82

Then all of a sudden Myrtle & Annie are extremely agitated.
They talk in whispers
and then in tears and
then in hands on hips and stomping.
It's about their club. "I can't stand it!" This is Annie.
"Just when we was getting so strong together,"
this is Myrtle. "I can't believe this is happening."

Their club is not my favorite topic. But naturally
I'm interested in their feelings of sadness;
what lifelong friend would not be?
They tell me with their high energy of anger:
"That church, it's not really Christian,
they disagree of the rules of our club,
their beliefs are wrong."
"Huh?" I say, as anybody would.
"The church where I saw your play?"
"No, LaVaughn, you didn't even listen,
we had to move two times since then," Annie tells me.

"This church was open arms to us,
and now they're kicking our club out,
and everybody in it," says Annie.
"Well, 'asking us'—
'asking us to leave' is what they say," says Myrtle.
"They say we are an impasse of negotiation,
and we don't even want to be in their church anyway,
they have wrong beliefs there,
they don't know Scripture like our leaders do,
they're false apostles like it says in the Bible.
Our leaders are so mad, they had a midnight meeting,
they're getting up a protest,
the church says our club is too extreme.
Too extreme? What's extreme about loving the Lord?"

Well.
I can only think of how it didn't seem right
from the very start.

"Everybody's mad, they're making posters,
getting ready for the rally. Come on, Annie,
we're supposed to *be* there," says Myrtle, "Bye, LaVaughn,"
and they go out the door fulminating.
A big word I learned from Dr. Rose
for being angry like a lightning strike.

And they surely did have their rally,
the police even came,
bottles and shoes got thrown through church windows,
and Myrtle & Annie's head shepherd
hit a policeman in the face with a Bible.

He went to jail.
It was even on the TV news, their club leaders yelling
about the Lord.

"Lordy," my mom says,
"the Joyful Universal Church of Jesus.
Myrtle & Annie really got themselves
into it this time, didn't they?" It looks horrible on the news.
I say, "Yeah, they did."

My mom puts her arm around my shoulders
and she kisses my neck.
"It's too bad, it's all too bad," she says.
"I thought they had more sense.
Bunch of fanatics." She huffs her breath out.

"But Myrtle & Annie didn't *know* that," I say.
My mom rolls her eyes.
I didn't even know if Myrtle & Annie
would come to my party after this. They could stay away
just from mere anger.

I was so scared when I saw the news about their rally
gone all crazy like that with people throwing things.
In my heart I was glad that club got broken up,
I felt myself smiling about it.
Boy, I can be so mean.
How does that happen?

83

But I was helpless with gratefulness
when Myrtle & Annie made their best birthday cake ever
for me
on such a sweltering day that everything melted
and the whole city lay down and got still.
Fire hydrants gushed in the streets that day
for children.

Myrtle & Annie brought me six "Jesus Loves You" balloons
and they floated above the room the whole afternoon.
"We still believe. We love the Lord more than ever now,
don't we, Myrtle?" Annie says, shoving the balloons
into my arms in generosity. Myrtle says she does, too.

The chocolate frosting
oozed and collapsed. Every window gaped open
into the sooty haze of the day,
the sweating, crowded refrigerator made moaning noises.
Ronell and the Brain Cells came in bringing food
and their good spirits

and Ronell even said, "Your house is *nice*."
She meant the curtains my mom made.
In a whoosh I discover I could tell her about Jody someday.
In Summer Science. On the bus. Maybe.

Doug brought a dozen party hats and tooter things
and a great big watermelon.
Doc jabbed his finger with the ice pick
trying to break up the ice,
and he was a good sport about it, bleeding only in the sink.

And in came Jolly's Ricky,
the amazing person who all by himself is teaching Jeremy
to read. Like everybody he is in shorts in this heat.
I see "Jolly" tattooed right above his bicep, on the left.
With poor Jolly's bad luck,
I wonder if he'll want it untattooed someday.

He's pushing Jilly in the stroller,
Jeremy hangs on the side like a big boy,
those huge eyes behind his glasses
sizing up the many new faces.
He found the toy earth mover I got him from Goodwill,
all washed up and clean
and he settles on the floor with it
like they belong together.
Jolly has a romance and he is here in the flesh
and I have a cut-up dancing dress in my closet.
Ricky picks Jilly up and holds her
while she grabs for the party streamers and watermelon.

Jolly tells me where she found Ricky:
She was walking the kids past some public grass,
and there was Ricky doing lawn work and flowers.

"And I had to keep nagging, Jeremy wouldn't keep up,
I was getting after him, 'Come *on,* Jeremy,'
you know how he looks at every little thing along the way.
And there he was, Ricky.
Down in the dirt with the flowers. Weeding, like.
And he said—
Go on, you tell her."
She shoulders Ricky's arm.

"Oh, I just said let the little one look at the flowers,
that's all." That's all he said.
He stood there, swaying with Jilly,
wiping her watermelon drool with his shirt.
Jolly said, "That's the way he is.
He ain't never raised a voice." Jolly, a slight hero
of her own life,
smiles at his elbow under Jilly's legs.
This Ricky even has quiet arms.
He folds up the stroller with one hand.
He looks like a refuge for Jolly. Yes. A refuge.
I don't think I ever thought of that word before.
And Patrick: He comes in,
this boy I laughed at,
now he brings me the fanciest bouquet, an armload of flowers,
but not like icky Lester. Patrick has written their botany names
by hand on little tags attached.
I put them in my father's ceramic pot.

I never knew anybody before that could even read those words.
giganticuaerulea, clusiana, spiraea thunbergii.
And I wouldn't know if they were spelled right or not.

Ronell sees the flowers and hoots,
"Woo-woo, LaVaughn!" and I introduce her to Patrick,
and it suddenly feels like a grown-up party: This is Ronell,
this is Patrick, they say Hi, Ronell even shakes his hand.
She looks him over, her eyes get interested.
"The Patrick? The Science Aptitude Test Patrick?
That's you?"
Patrick pretends he didn't hear her, he looks away.
"Yeah, this is that guy," I say.
"You! Woo, Patrick."
And she settles in beside him.

All these party guests
are eating melon and chips, saying they never
had better potato salad
than my mom made a huge mass of.
And she keeps her promise
about staying away from the party.

My team of Brain Cells cheered the loudest
when I blew out all 16 candles
with Jeremy helping,
leaning way over from the kitchen stool,
hoping it was his birthday too.
Myrtle & Annie grinned
when everybody said their cake was so excellent.
It was maybe the best thing they had all week,

with their club all in chaos
and nothing to do in the afternoons.

They prayed before they ate their food
as if they went into a secret room for a minute,
leaving us behind by their closed eyes and perched hands.

Jilly gets around, making friends.
Doc carries her all around the party table on his shoulders,
bumping into "Jesus Loves You" balloons,
and Jilly's little bare feet keep time on his chest
while everyone claps in rhythm.

I kept thinking how I seem to be regular,
a person having a party
like real life. And in my room is a dry, leathery rose
that is too embarrassing to admit.
And yet I keep it there like a flag.
There were presents.
I didn't ask for any, but here they were.
Myrtle & Annie gave me a package
wrapped in about ten bows and curlicues.
Inside was a Bible, with gold lettering on the front,
and a little book, *The Lord Is My Saturday Night Date.*
I thanked them in our old friendly code way,
they meant it from their hearts.

Jeremy sits on the kitchen stool
pulled up close to the party table,
coloring in the *Little Scientist Coloring Book* that Doc gave me
along with the 64 crayons.

I unwrap the gift Ronell and Doug brought:
It's a baseball cap that says,
"Everything you can imagine is real."
"Turn it around," says Ronell, nudging it over
on my hand. On the back it says "(Picasso)."
"The artist, you know?" Ronell says,
and I put the hat on,
Doug and Ronell go into the bathroom with me
to see how it looks in the mirror.
Party noises roll through the rooms.

Even Jolly. I turn around and there's a package
wrapped in newspaper with a big red ribbon,
and it has my name on it,
and the word "fragl."
I open it up and inside is a flat piece of clay
with handprints in it,
one little and one tiny.
Their names, Jeremy and Jilly, are scratched straight
underneath the handprints, maybe with a matchstick.
I think how many times I washed their handprints
off the walls in Jolly's sad house
and now they are my birthday present.
"Ricky, he showed them how to make that," she says.
I thank Jolly and I know she would never catch on
how those handprints will make my private bedroom
a better place.

84

And then what happened.
What happened.

It was simple enough at the surface.
I was down under the table, on my hands and knees
mopping up the cake and ice cream
that fell off Jilly's plate
so the ants wouldn't gather on it.
I had done this wiping for Jilly so many times before,
it felt good to be connected back
with that little dear girl in my life
who has such health and bright eyes
even with her poor, bad-luck mom.

But there was a sudden break in the talk
up above me, a slight lift of breath.
Someone was coming in the door, I heard it unlock.
Not my mom. Voices stopped in the middle of a word
or laugh, and then went on.
A moment of pause, that was all,
like a brief question mark
and I could feel people's laps tense under the table

256

and then relax. Just an instant, only that long.
Something new was in the room.

I must have turned around under there.
Standing right in my face were the bare feet and legs
I had memorized,
legs I would never forget, each muscle curve and incline.

And a voice, Jeremy's:
"LaBon down dere, down dere, down dere,"
a song above the voices,
and I watched like a slow movie
as the legs bent and squatted down
and I was looking straight
into Jody's face
under the table, my hand full of wet rag and
ice cream and cake mess
and Jeremy singing up above,
"LaBon down dere, down dere."

Jody held out a big flat package in a bright pink ribbon,
he looked straight in my face.
I would never forget the eerie perfection of his eyes.

All the things I could have done.
Smear the mop-up rag on his face
to pay him back for such hurting.
Cover my own face with the hanging paper tablecloth,
making him as invisible
as he had been for weeks.
Kiss him with my whole heart.
I don't move or breathe. Jody doesn't flinch.

He smiles at me a little bit,
pushing the birthday gift into my hands
as if this was any afternoon in the world.
I can't resist his eyes, my fist loosens on the dripping rag,
it drops. I wipe my hand on my shorts.

And it came to me down there on the floor
how it was not just Jody
that was making me so miserable. It was
my not forgiving him
for being Jody
that was the worst,
weighting me down. I put my hand on the package.

All those legs around me, everybody
with their sadness about their lives
but having a good time anyway.
The Brain Cells who work so hard to climb,
Patrick who's forgiven me,
Myrtle & Annie
baking my birthday cake even being mad at me.
Jilly beating her bare feet on the phone books
right near my forehead, alive as she can be.
Jeremy singing, kneeling on the kitchen stool.
And Jolly: no history at all she even knew about,
nobody to care about her except random people
that turned up from surprise places.
Jolly, a forgotten person, a throwaway girl,
was laughing and eating cake
with her two fatherless children
and I was going to die because the boyfriend I want
doesn't want a girlfriend.

The guests were all laughing up there
above my head and Jody's.
And I saw in all that bundle of legs
I was ridiculous. And my angry, hurt heart
made a little relaxing noise
that nobody could hear but me.
Dr. Rose: It wasn't that horrible moment
back then, that horrifying day. It was *this* one.
"We must make momentous decisions."
I knew I could keep
freezing myself away from Jody
pretending I could change him
or I could quit doing that.

Jody lets go of the package in my hands.
It's heavy. I stroke it first, I can't help it.
Then I undo the ribbon
and the paper folds back
and there is a book there.
A shiny picture of marble human beings
and in big letters, MICHELANGELO.
I open it. It's full of sculptures
and paintings all over the ceiling in Rome.
"Jody," I say. It's the first time I have said his name
above a whisper in so long.
"Happy Birthday, LaVaughn.
He painted on the ceiling, too."
My whole nervous system jumps for an instant
then settles down inside me again
and it feels like my own right heart
being sorry and sad and happy and glad and nervy
and mine.

I inhale and I say, "Thank you."
And he shrugs. And he blinks.
Under the table there
he leans over and kisses me on the cheek.
Dr. Rose comes back to me
and I get it. I get it. I get it!
We will rise to the occasion
which is life.

I scrinch out from under the table
leaving the mopping rag down there,
holding my new book in my arm.
Jody too backs out and
crawling like crabs
we stand up.
I reach down and take Jody's hand,
braver than I would ever think myself to be,
and I say, an announcement,
"This is my friend Jody."
I am holding his hand,
he is holding mine,
and for an instant moment in my own house
it makes sense.

I could never explain it.

There is another slight intake of breath around the table,
and then Doc says, "Yo, Jody, have some cake."

85

I look around at the party
to have it by memory forever.
Jilly has a paper streamer wound around herself
and chocolate cake in her hair.
She climbs down off the phone books and
picks up Jeremy's toy truck,
and Ricky is right there to play with her,
pushing the truck under chairs
with sound effects.

Jilly has no idea
how nearly dead she was that day
last year when everything seemed to be over.
And I suddenly know why
I didn't want to get a cat with Myrtle.
It's not only the smell. It's the purring cat itself:
You get to love the little thing
and then it could die.
Loving is so dangerous.

Ricky helps Jeremy wash his hands
and then Jeremy sits on Doc's lap
to look at my new Michelangelo book,
Doc's finger is bandaged from the ice pick.
Doug is getting more punch from the fridge
and pouring it out for people.

Jody is on the kitchen stool
talking with Myrtle about their Egyptian mummies
from sixth grade and they are laughing
with fingers in their noses,
remembering how the brains got sucked out.
And here's Annie:
She's licked the candle she took out of her piece of cake
and lined it up with her fork on the paper plate.
Annie has always been the neatest one.
She and Jolly and Ronell are holding a conversation
and it seems to be about shoes.
I hear her invite Ronell to a club meeting
when they get a new place to meet
but I can't hear what Ronell says in return
with the tooting of the tooters around the table.

Annie looks over at me and says with her eyes and her head
in code, as we have always spoken:
"You didn't invite Jody! He crashed your party!"
I say with my eyes and head back to her,
"Yeah, Annie, he crashed. He is my friend."

How much that book of pictures must have cost.
Jody spent his college money on it.

Dear God, will I ever understand anything?
Patrick's flowers with their long Latin name tags
are in my father's pot.
I have been punishing him for so long
for not being Jody. I go over to where he is
watching Ricky and Jilly on the floor
and I say, "I appreciate the flowers, Patrick."
He says, "I thought you would."
Patrick looks at Jody and me, back and forth.
I imagine he knows about my insane heart.
With his smart mind, I'm sure he knows.
The whole embarrassing terrible thing.

I go to the kitchen to get a sponge
for the chocolate cake marks on the wall
at Jilly's height. When my mom comes home
those marks have to be gone.

I know I should open up the card
attached to the dead brown pink rose in my room
and read it some day.

I put suds on the sponge
and I head for the wall.
Jeremy is wearing my new hat,
and he sings "Happy Birthday LaBon" in his own tune.
The party seems like a miracle,
happening out of all desperate misery.
My slashed dancing dress is in my closet,
the rotting orange still in my room.
Jeremy comes over to me, puts his arms around my leg

and hangs there, his head against my thigh.
I look at Jody and he looks back at me.
The look is quick as a blink,
the whole world is going by outside.

This is the way it has turned out.
I feast my eyes on this amazing birthday
and I think I can live with the way life is.
I say in my heart,
Guy, your daughter is sixteen.
How do you feel about that?